IT'S NOT YOU,
IT'S ME

GABRIELLE WILLIAMS

ALLEN&UNWIN
SYDNEY・MELBOURNE・AUCKLAND・LONDON

First published by Allen & Unwin in 2021

Copyright © Text, Gabrielle Williams 2021
Copyright © Cover Illustration, Kim Ekdahl 2021

All rights reserved. No part of this book may be reproduced or transmitted
in any form or by any means, electronic or mechanical, including
photocopying, recording or by any information storage and retrieval
system, without prior permission in writing from the publisher. The
Australian *Copyright Act 1968* (the Act) allows a maximum of one chapter
or ten per cent of this book, whichever is the greater, to be photocopied
by any educational institution for its educational purposes provided
that the educational institution (or body that administers it) has given a
remuneration notice to the Copyright Agency (Australia) under the Act.

Allen & Unwin
83 Alexander Street
Crows Nest NSW 2065
Australia
Phone: (61 2) 8425 0100
Email: info@allenandunwin.com
Web: www.allenandunwin.com

 A catalogue record for this
book is available from the
National Library of Australia

ISBN 978 1 76052 607 8

For teaching resources, explore www.allenandunwin.com/resources/for-teachers

Cover and text design by Sandra Nobes
Cover artwork by Kim Ekdahl
Pages i and iii artwork by Kim Ekdahl
Page vii diagram created by Gabrielle Williams, set by Sandra Nobes
Set in 11/18 pt Adobe Caslon Pro by Midland Typesetters, Australia
Printed in Australia by McPherson's Printing Group

10 9 8 7 6 5 4 3 2 1

 The paper in this book is FSC® certified.
FSC® promotes environmentally responsible,
socially beneficial and economically viable
management of the world's forests.

🐦 @gab_williams
📷 @gabwilliamswrites

For Andrew, Nique,
Harry and Charlie xxxx

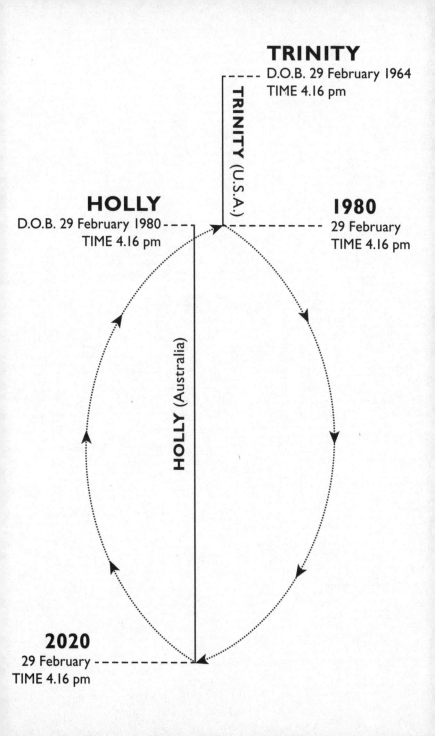

TRINITY
D.O.B. 29 February 1964
TIME 4.16 pm

TRINITY (U.S.A.)

HOLLY
D.O.B. 29 February 1980
TIME 4.16 pm

1980
29 February
TIME 4.16 pm

HOLLY (Australia)

2020
29 February
TIME 4.16 pm

Day 1

**FRIDAY,
29 FEBRUARY
1980**

Holly

4.16 pm

This is what Holly Fitzgerald knew for sure: She'd been out for lunch. She'd come home. She'd gone inside. End of story.

So she was having trouble figuring out what she was doing lying on a nature strip, staring up at the sky, blades of grass pricking against her wrists and the backs of her legs. Her bones felt bruised. She suspected there was a very big chance she would tip out the entire contents of her queasy stomach if she lifted her head off the ground.

There was a gap where her memory was supposed to fit.

She remembered sitting at lunch, celebrating turning forty, toasting the new decade. Like turning forty and 2020 were good things. So far (and it was only February): her best friend had died; millions of hectares of bush had burned in worst-in-a-century bushfires; a thing called coronavirus was sweeping the world; people were saying Australia might have to go into 'lockdown' (whatever that meant); and just to make the perfect start to the perfect year even more perfect, her boyfriend had gone off to Sydney for a golfing long weekend and was missing her birthday altogether.

And now here she was, lying face-up on the footpath.

Her senses prickled with strangeness: strange smells, strange sounds, strange light. She struggled up onto her elbows, keeping her stomach in check by a sheer effort of will.

The street was quiet, the neighbourhood unfamiliar, the house styles varied: a Californian bungalow here, a white two-storey there, a Spanish hacienda on the other side of the road. On a busy main drag visible beyond the corner a few metres to her right, traffic was bumper to bumper. Except all the cars were long and boaty, like from America in the seventies. And they were all driving on the wrong side of the road.

A young guy leant into her field of vision. 'Trinity?' he said. 'You okay?'

Add strange person calling her a strange name to the mix.

Holly looked down the length of her body. She was wearing a faded pink T-shirt with 'Disco Sux' written across the front of it. Her legs poked out of a pair of cut-off denim shorts, and she was wearing black Converse runners. But none of them were hers. The canvas runners, the T-shirt (she *liked* disco), the shorts, the legs…all of them belonged to someone else.

She sat all the way up and went to put her head in her hands, to cover her eyes, to think for a moment, but her hands weren't hers either. These ones were smaller than she was used to. The nail polish was baby blue.

She'd just turned forty. She didn't do baby-blue nails.

Holly wiggled the fingers to make sure she could operate them; turned the palms towards her, then away again.

'What are you doing?' the young guy asked her.

She'd forgotten he was there. Time felt clunky and pulled out of shape, as if one thing didn't necessarily follow straight on from another.

'My hands,' she said, holding them up to him in explanation.

'What about them?' the young guy asked.

'Look at them.'

He clasped them for a couple of seconds. 'They're clammy,' he said, staring at her. 'Trinity, are you okay? What happened?'

She had no idea why he was calling her Trinity, but as she stared back at him a name came into her brain. She had insight. Clarity. Knowledge.

'Lewis,' she said, clicking her fingers and pointing them gun-like at him.

'Yeah?'

'You live next door.'

'Yeah.' He stretched the word out like bubblegum, stalling for time, before asking again, third time lucky, 'Are you okay?'

Holly thought for a moment, giving the question due consideration. 'Uh...no, not really.'

Understatement of the century. Or technically (as it would turn out), understatement of two centuries.

'You wanna stand up?' Lewis asked, hauling her up onto her feet.

As she stood up, a hank of long blonde hair fell

forward, the tips dyed black. She grabbed it and brought it up in front of her eyes; turned the hair over, watched the light catch on it. It was cut into layers, soft, shiny, pretty, pale, the black edge in stark contrast.

'My hair,' she said, holding it out to him.

'Yeah?'

'It's not mine.'

Lewis shook his head as if he didn't quite get the joke.

In fact, now that she was starting to get her bearings she noticed that her voice didn't sound like hers either.

Dizziness overwhelmed her and she sat back down on the nature strip, her legs not fit to hold her upright. Lewis squatted back down beside her, concern all over his features.

There was a lag between what she was seeing and hearing, and the fact of it settling into her brain. How could her hair not be hers? Her legs, her hands, her fingernails. Her voice. Why were the cars on the wrong side of the road? Where *was* she? How had she got here?

Lewis reached over and picked up a fringed suede shoulder bag that was lying on the ground close by. Handed it to her. Handed her a pair of mirror-lensed Aviator sunglasses that had been lying next to it. She took them both, simply because she didn't have the energy to explain that they weren't hers, and opened the bag. Inside was: a leather purse with flowers embossed on it, a pack of cigarettes (without the gruesome health warning or accompanying photo), a Zippo lighter, a Ray-Ban glasses case, and a thin book of poetry by Walt Whitman.

No phone.

And by the way, going back to the fact of cigarettes... this definitely wasn't her bag.

She put her hands up to her eyes, pushing blackness into her vision. She just wanted to be home, surrounded by things she recognised. Her own hands and legs, at the bare minimum.

'I'm sorry, I don't know what's going on. Can you call me an Uber?' she said, keeping her hands over her eyes, trying to steady herself.

'A what?'

'An Uber. I just want to get home.'

'Home?' Lewis said, then nothing more.

Holly looked up to see him pointing to a house a couple of doors down the quiet street. He seemed to be indicating that it was her house, but it wasn't. It definitely wasn't. For one thing, it wasn't on her street, and surely your most basic expectation was that your house would be on your street.

Lewis stood up and held out his hand to bring her back up level with him.

She looked up at him, frustration overwhelming her, wanting to yell, *No, you don't understand, that's not my house, this isn't my neighbourhood, it's not my name, what are you talking about, you don't even know me.*

But it was exhausting to even contemplate saying so many words out loud. Besides, there was something about Lewis that this body trusted. Holly could feel it in her slowly settling guts.

So she abdicated all responsibility over to the unfamiliar body she found herself in, and let him bring her back up to standing. Together, hand in hand, they walked towards the house he'd pointed at.

There was a neat green lawn with a concrete path cutting straight through its centre, from footpath to verandah. The verandah was big and breezy and cast a deep shadow over the front windows. The roof was broad and shingled, with a large attic window. Rising out of the lawn on the right-hand side was an enormous pine tree with a gnarly trunk, and down the left ran a driveway.

It was not her weatherboard Victorian with tiny front yard and no room for a driveway.

Absolutely not her house.

4.28 pm

Holly knew, even before Lewis pushed open the door, that the entrance hall would be decorated in tones of burgundy and brown. A teak hallway table would have an owl lamp on it (whenever letters arrived for anyone in the house, they'd be put under the owl's feet). A black plastic telephone with a push-button dial would be sitting beside the owl lamp, a curly cord connecting to its receiver. Beside the phone would be a Teledex containing handwritten phone numbers and addresses for friends and family, school and work. There'd be a lounge room with a fireplace and a couch covered with geometric gold-and-cream fabric; a dining table and chairs with matching skinny black spider-legs. Along one wall would be an upright piano, and on the floor, burnt-orange carpet. Stairs would lead up to the second storey, where the bedrooms would be.

She followed Lewis into the house, and there it all was: the teak table, the owl lamp, the black phone, the Teledex, burnt-orange carpet, spider-leg table and chairs, piano. Everything utterly familiar and utterly unfamiliar, all at the same time.

Lewis was watching her reaction. 'There was a guy,' he said. 'When I came out of my joint, he was trying to lift you into his car. Do you remember?'

Off the lounge room would be a kitchen with bright-orange laminate cupboards, a breakfast table with bench seats, a fridge with a pull-out handle. She could even picture the box of Frosted Flakes that would be inside the cupboard above the sink.

A bowl of cereal with ice-cold milk would really hit the spot right about now. Except Holly didn't do sugary crap. Didn't rely on cartoon tigers on cereal boxes for her dietary choices.

'I asked him what was going on,' Lewis was saying, 'and he said you'd fainted and he was going to drive you home. But I pointed to your house and said, "Except she lives there," and then he just dumped you on the ground and got in his car and drove off.'

Holly approached the staircase and started climbing it, slowly, feeling like an intruder but knowing no one would stop her. This was her home. Even though it wasn't. The banister felt well-worn and comfortable under her hand. There was a slight nick in the wood that her palm recognised.

She could sense Lewis's eyes at her back; his confusion, knowing something was wrong, but unable to pinpoint exactly what it was. Of course he couldn't. Who could?

'You want me to make some toast or something?' Lewis called up after her. 'I'll make us toast,' he decided.

At the upstairs landing was a hallway. Holly knew that to her left were the bedrooms. To her right was the bathroom. She turned left, feeling a fluttering inside her chest like a bird was trapped in there.

In the first bedroom, the wallpaper was an assault of oversized yellow sunflowers, red and orange tulips, green leaves. Ditto the curtains and the lampshade, with the same pattern. A poster of Debbie Harry wearing sunglasses and a black beret was stuck to one wall, along with cut-outs from magazine pages. There was a single bed, unmade. Yellow carpet – not that you could see much of it, considering the clothes and books and general crap strewn everywhere. A blue-and-white striped bath towel dumped on the floor. A milk crate tipped onto its side, vinyl records spilling out. A bashed-up acoustic guitar in the corner. And then the one thing that Holly was not expecting to see: on the desk under the window, an orange enamel typewriter. A shiny, new orange enamel Brother 210 typewriter.

The one familiar thing in all this strangeness.

'I found it at this vintage shop,' Evie had said, at lunch that day, 'and I thought it was perfect for you.' As Holly unwrapped her present, Evie went on, 'And even more perfect, the guy told me it was made in late seventy-nine, which makes it forty. And now here you are, turning forty. It's forty. You're forty. You two were made for each other. Happy birthday!'

Holly had run her fingers over the smooth orange enamel, marred only by a slight scratch on the top left panel. She'd grinned up at Evie. 'I love it. It's perfect.' She loved that Evie knew her so well that she'd take a punt on a strange gift like a vintage orange Brother typewriter, and get it a hundred per cent right.

Holly stepped over the mess to the desk. Stared down at the typewriter. Ran a finger over a slight scratch in the top left panel. It couldn't be. The orange enamel was glossy. The keys were glistening, sharp black with pristine white letters stamped on them.

It was the fresh-out-of-the-box version of the one Evie had given her earlier that afternoon.

The minute she got home she'd set it up on her desk in the front room. The typewriter sat there, like, 'gimme paper'. So she'd scrolled in a piece of white A4, then wondered what to type. Her fingers rested on the keys, trying to find the starting words. She decided on a 'thank you for my typewriter' letter to Evie.

Dear, she typed, then stopped.

The ink on the ribbon was so dry the letters barely registered on the page. It was as if the lifeblood of the typewriter itself had been drained. She needed to get a new ribbon.

But now that she'd started, she wanted to try it out, hear the clack as the keys pressed down, the clatter as the metal letter arms slapped up towards the page. She could tell, even from having typed a single short word, that it required a different touch to a laptop. Heavier. Firmer. Each letter pressed deliberately.

So, what to write? Dear who?

She looked at the still-vibrant orange enamel, the Brother logo in the top left panel, and suddenly her fingers were tapping out:

Dear Brother Orange

The next thing she knew, she was waking up on the footpath out the front. And now, here was the typewriter, the exact one, on the desk under the window in this bedroom, brand new, with a sheet of paper wound into it. Holly yanked the page up and stared at the typescript – black as coal, standing out loud and proud against the white page.

Dear Brother Orange

Holly felt dizzy. She plonked down onto the bed, putting her head in her hands again. She needed to get out of here. But where would she go? Nothing made sense. She wondered if her drink had been spiked at lunch. It was possible. But surely even if you were completely drugged out of your brain, you'd recognise your own home, your own hands, your legs, your hair, when you came to?

This wasn't drugs. This was something else entirely.

'You got no butter,' she heard someone calling up the stairs. 'I'll go grab some from our joint.'

A vague waft of toast-air brought her back to the room she was in. Lewis. How did she know his name? And when he'd called her Trinity, she'd known it was her name the moment he'd said it – had felt the rightness of it deep down in her chest.

She wasn't her. She was someone else altogether. Which made no sense. Conversely, it was the only thing that made sense.

A simple look in the full-length mirror that she knew was on the inside of the wardrobe door would surely prove her hunch right. But the thought of an unfamiliar face staring back at her filled her with a heavy dread. She chewed down on her thumbnail, a habit she hadn't indulged in for a very long time, and found that there wasn't much to chew on; these nails had already been well and truly gnawed.

To get away from the mirror behind the door, Holly walked out of the bedroom and into the hallway, towards the rest of the bedrooms. Checking that all was as she had it mapped out inside her head.

The first bedroom had a double bed neatly made up with a quilt of peach velour, floral carpet, glass doors opening onto a small balcony, built-in robes. The parents' room. Check. Exactly as she'd expected.

She crossed the hallway to the other bedroom, which followed a similar theme to hers – a chaotic floral design (pink, this time) covering the walls, curtains, lampshades, chest of drawers, quilt cover. Except in this instance, the quilt was pulled up neatly, the pillows plumped, the clothes put away. Everything was ordered and pristine. The way Holly preferred things.

On the bed, leaning against the pillow, was a soft-bodied ragdoll with blonde plaits, big round eyes and a small stitched mouth, wearing a patchwork pinafore and a cloth bonnet, its arms folded across its lap. A Holly Hobbie doll. Holly had the exact same one herself, given to her when she was born. It was her namesake. Even now, it was in her hallway cupboard, boxed up with all the sentimental bits and bobs she'd never been able to get rid of: a stack of old photos, the letter her dad had written to her mum, Grannie Aileen's mahjong set.

Loolah. That was the name of the little girl whose bedroom this was.

Holly put her baby-blue fingernails in her mouth and chewed. She knew what she had to do next. She couldn't put it off any longer.

She walked out of the pink bedroom and faced the bathroom door at the other end of the hallway. The wall tiles would be blue, with some pink feature panels, and the sink, bath and toilet would be white. The floor tiles would be a deep burgundy red, and there would be a fern in a pot on the edge of the bath. She'd put a million bucks on it. And she knew exactly what the face in the mirror over the sink would look like.

A wave of clamminess washed over her. There would be no going back once she'd seen herself. But she had to know.

She walked slowly down the hallway to the bathroom then over to the sink and stared into the mirror.

Sure enough, an unfamiliar face blinked back at her, but it was also completely and utterly familiar. The eyes were grey, rimmed with black eyeliner, the long lashes slathered in mascara. There was a flush of pink on the cheeks. The mouth was neat, the hair messy: blonde, black-tipped, the fringe falling down over her eyes. The nose was long, but somehow it seemed to be the ideal length for the face. The cheekbones were angular, cutting in diagonally from the tops of her ears. The jaw was square, strong. The eyebrows winged up, as if this girl was permanently quizzical. The left ear was pierced up the flank with six keepers and one hoop, the right with one silver stud.

A phone started ringing down the hall in the parents' bedroom. Also in the kitchen downstairs. And on the hallway table, under the owl lamp. She knew exactly where each phone was. Had sat talking for hours on each of them.

Holly didn't move, transfixed by the mirror. She heard a click, and then the voice of a woman, older, echoing through the house – 'You've called the Byrne residence. We're not home at the moment. Please leave a message...' – followed by a beep to let the caller know the tape was lined up and ready to record.

Byrne. That was the surname of this girl. Of this body she now found herself in. Trinity Byrne.

Except her name was Holly Fitzgerald and today was her fortieth birthday.

But no. It wasn't. She was this girl. Trinity Byrne.

And seriously, what the actual hell.

5.07 pm

Holly knelt on the floor of the yellow bedroom flipping through the photo albums that she'd pulled out of the bookcase, trying to grasp her place in this world.

There was a photo of her with her arm slung over the shoulder of another girl: Susie Sioux, that was this girl's name. There was a photo of Lewis, skateboard in hand, looking like he might tease you or kiss you, hadn't decided yet. There was a girl wearing a full-length pink rabbit outfit crouched in the front yard of a house – April. Sometimes they called her Aprilmayjune.

Last year they'd cut class, Susie Sioux and Aprilmayjune and Trinity, to go to the cinema and see Big Wednesday. *The lights went down, the film started: lots of underwater footage, as you might expect from a surf movie. But as the intro rolled on, Aprilmayjune had whispered, 'I don't think this is* Big Wednesday,' *and then the iconic theme music started up and a shark attacked the skindivers and it clicked that they were in* Jaws 2, *and the three of them burst out laughing, sneaking out and running into the right cinema, proceeding to giggle uncontrollably at inappropriate moments all through* Big Wednesday, *one of them remembering the whole wrong-cinema thing, trying to suppress a laugh, and setting the others off like dominoes.*

Holly turned the page onto another photo of Aprilmayjune; in this one she was laughing her head off as she lay on the lap of some guy, more guys piled on top of her. In another, a boy was shimmying up a pole and reaching out to the camera, a cigarette between his teeth. There was a photo of a girl with a can of shaving cream, spraying a foam love heart on a bathroom mirror around the name 'David'. Girls piled on the bed in this crazy yellow bedroom. A girl and a guy kissing, a hand held up to the camera to give them some privacy.

A group, maybe twenty in total, lying on the beach, bodies brown, bathers brief, cigarettes between fingers. A guy leaning out a car window, hand raised to shield his eyes from the sun.

Booze. Houses. Parties. Gardens. Cars.

Holly remembered it all. She'd been at all these places. These were her friends: Susie Sioux and April and Lewis and Heather and Jennifer and Amy, Robbie and Kevin and Eric and Scott. All these names that came to her without any prompting.

She heard a noise and looked up to see Lewis standing in the doorway, two plates in his hand. She'd forgotten all about him.

'I have jam,' he said, holding up one plate, 'or peanut butter,' and he held up the other plate. 'But not together.' And he swooshed the plates over each other, back and forth, like a magician. 'Because I still can't get my head around the whole peanut-butter-and-jelly thing. Separate. Always gotta be separate.'

He looked over her shoulder at the photo album lying open on the floor. There was a picture of the two of them, Trinity and Lewis, at a park, her sitting on a skateboard laughing at something happening to her right, him standing behind looking down at her.

He squatted, put the plates on the floor, and dragged the album towards him. Grinned. 'That's when I'd just arrived from Oz, yeah?' He picked up a piece of toast with jam and shoved it in his mouth.

Holly clicked her fingers. 'Australia,' she said.

'Yeah. What?' he asked.

'You're Australian.'

He shook his head at her. 'Trin, what's going on?' he said. 'You reckon your hair isn't yours. You don't know which one's your house. A guy tries to put you in his car. You suddenly remember I'm from Australia. I don't get it.'

Holly chewed on her bottom lip, a habit, she could tell, of this girl she now was. 'Well...' The word peeled slowly out of her mouth as her brain swung between two options: tell him the truth, or stall for time. She thought back over the past half-hour or so, all the things she didn't understand, the hands, legs, hair, body that wasn't hers. She looked over at Lewis: what *was* she trying to say? What even was the truth? Stalling for time seemed the better option. 'It's just that sometimes I can really hear it in your voice.' She picked up a piece of toast with peanut butter and tore off a crust, then put it into her mouth.

'On top of all that,' Lewis went on, 'you still haven't told me who that guy was, and why he was trying to put you in his car. He was literally carrying you. You're acting like it didn't happen.'

Looking at the curve of his neck, the line of his jaw, the length of his eyelashes, Holly felt a sting of how beautiful life was when you were young and had your entire future in front of you. She wondered about his relationship with Trinity. Were they just friends? He lived next door, she knew that much. But everything else was still blurred, frustratingly out of reach.

She looked away from him, suddenly conscious of how much she didn't know about this life she was in.

'I don't know what happened,' she finally said. 'I don't know why I was lying on the footpath. I don't remember anything until when I woke up.'

Lewis stared at her. '"Footpath"?'

'Yes. Out the front.'

'"Footpath"?' he repeated. 'Really?'

'Yeah. What's your point?'

'Since when do you call it a footpath? I don't think there's an American alive who even knows what a footpath is.'

Holly looked away from him, down at her hands. Trinity's hands. No, her hands. She was Trinity Byrne, and this was her house, and these were her hands. She brought her thumbnail up to her mouth and chewed it again.

'Well, that's what you call it, isn't it?' she said, her thumb acting as a barrier, keeping her safe from his questions. 'In Australia? I was trying to be, you know, Australian. I was joking. It was a joke.'

'I call it a sidewalk,' he said. 'Because that's what it's called over here.'

He stared at her, obviously about to say more, but then the front door downstairs opened, and a voice called, 'Hi hon, you home?'

Holly felt her entire body run hot and then cold and then flare hot again. It was her mum. Her mom. Trinity's mom.

She stood up, the photo albums, the footpath conversation, the toast, all of it forgotten, and ran out of the bedroom, down the stairs, and into the kitchen where she stopped in her tracks, her hands gripping the doorjamb as she stared at the woman unpacking a brown paper bag of groceries.

The woman was wearing a blue nurse's uniform, a belt cinched at the waist. Beside her was a little girl of nine or ten rummaging inside another bag of groceries before taking out what she'd been looking for – a packet of biscuits. She tore open the packaging and slotted one into her mouth.

Trinity's mom and her little sister, Loolah.

Holly felt like she was all metal, and this mother and sister were all magnet. She walked over to them, wanted to be close to them, to hug them, but then she was overcome by her own fakery. She wasn't really this person; she wasn't meant to be here. She took a step back.

'How's your day been?' the mom said, a throwaway comment, casual, relaxed, like standing here together in this kitchen wasn't even a big deal.

Holly was unable to put together even the simplest answer, not so much as the word 'good'.

'Did anyone do anything for your birthday?' the little girl, Loolah, asked through her biscuit-chomping. Then she added, 'Oh, hey Lewis,' with a half-raised hand.

Holly stared at her. 'My birthday?' she said sharply.

The mom stopped unpacking. Loolah stared back at Holly. Holly could feel Lewis at her back, his energy focused on her.

'Yeah,' Loolah repeated. 'Your birthday. Sixteen. Today. What? Weirdo.'

Holly opened her mouth, but her brain was whirring, processing this new information. She felt paralysed. So it was this body's birthday today as well.

'Trinity,' the mom said, the name snapping Holly out of her unsteadiness. 'Are you all right?'

Holly looked around the kitchen. Loolah was still staring at her. So were the mom and Lewis. She looked away from them, willing them to stop, wanting to convince them that everything was normal here. *This is me, I'm your daughter, your sister, your friend, everything's as it's supposed to be.* She picked up the just-opened packet of biscuits and turned to Lewis. 'Biscuit?'

The silence in the kitchen got heavier, if that was even possible.

And then Holly realised. 'Cookie,' she corrected.

She turned away, still avoiding the three sets of eyes. And that's when she noticed the newspaper sitting on the breakfast bench. *Los Angeles Times*, said the gothic masthead.

She'd figured out already that she was somewhere in America, what with all the cars, the accents, the cookies. But...okay, so Los Angeles. The date – *29 February 1980* –

was written underneath the masthead in small type, like it barely mattered. Like it was the most banal of information.

The packet of biscuits slipped from her grasp, landing on the bench beside the newspaper.

Holly was born on 29 February 1980.

29 February 1980 was Trinity's sixteenth birthday.

Somehow, she'd been dropped into the life of a whole other leap-year baby.

Oh, and one more thing: Holly had been born in Los Angeles.

Mind.

Officially.

Blown.

5.52 pm

'I don't get what's going on,' Lewis said as he departed through the front doorway, shaking his head back at Holly. 'Maybe that guy did something. You should tell your mom what happened. In case you've been, I don't know, something?'

It seemed strange that he was using 'mom', instead of the Australian 'mum'. But he used 'sidewalk' instead of 'footpath'. He'd obviously been here long enough to instinctively use Americanisms, but not so long that he'd lost his accent.

'Something's not right,' he added.

No shit, Sherlock.

Personally, Holly thought she'd been handling the situation fantastically well so far, all things considered. But he had a point. Things were definitely not right. Maybe now was the time for that old chestnut: the truth. Now that she knew a bit more about what was going on.

She ran through the truth inside her head to hear how it would sound.

You know what, Lewis, you're totally correct. Something's definitely not right. For some inexplicable reason I've woken up to find myself in the body of a sixteen-year-old girl, who happens to be a leap-year baby like me. That woman in the kitchen who's supposed to be my mum? Wait, my 'mom'. And that little girl? Never seen either of them before in my life. Of course peanut butter doesn't go with jelly. And by the way, we both know it's 'jam' not 'jelly'. And that guy who you say was trying to put me in his car? Maybe he's a friend, maybe he was trying to help, maybe he's a bad guy. I don't know anything about him. Oh, and one other thing: I come from the future. From 2020.

Yeah, she didn't need to go terribly far down the track of truth to know it wasn't an option.

But he was right. She needed to tell the mom something – come up with some kind of alibi that would excuse all the wrong-footed things she kept saying. Calling cookies biscuits, that type of thing. Because she couldn't imagine it getting any easier. She couldn't just slot into a stranger's life and not trip up.

(It wasn't even worth getting into the 'why' of what was going on, at the moment. Better to deal with the 'is' of it and make the best of the situation.)

Holly shut the door behind Lewis and went back into the kitchen. The mom was stirring a pot on the cooktop. (Which, by the way, smelt delicious. Holly realised she was *starving*.) She watched the mom for a moment, gathering up her courage, then – trying for nonchalance, no big deal – said, 'Something happened this afternoon.'

The mom turned and looked at her, the wooden spoon still stirring. 'Hm?'

'I'm not sure what, exactly,' Holly went on. 'All I know is, I woke up and I was lying on the foot— sidewalk out the front and Lewis was standing over me, and he said some guy had been trying to put me into his car.'

The mom stopped stirring. 'What do you mean, some guy was trying to put you in his car?' she asked.

Holly put her hands up in the universal symbol of 'don't panic'. 'It's fine. I'm fine,' she added. 'It's just...that's what Lewis said.'

'What did he look like?'

'The guy? I don't know.'

'What sort of car was he driving?'

'I don't know.'

The mom frowned. 'Okay, let's start at the beginning. What happened?'

'I don't know.'

The mom shook her head and sighed. Not a gentle, calming sigh – an exasperated, what-the-fuck sigh. 'All right, well, can you at least tell me where you were headed?' she asked, her mouth a grim line. 'You're grounded, in case you've forgotten.'

'Grounded?'

'Yes. Last week. Or don't you know that either?' There was a definite tinge of sarcasm in the mom's voice now.

There'd been a rat-a-tat of bony knuckles on the front door. Trinity, upstairs in her bedroom, heard footsteps below, then indistinct talking for a moment before Mom called for her to come downstairs. Mrs Glickman was standing on the front porch, looking smug and self-satisfied. Righteous. Trinity knew exactly what this was all about.

'Mrs Glickman says she picked you up hitchhiking earlier today,' Mom said. 'But I told her you'd never hitchhike – would you?' *Trinity glared at Mrs Glickman in response, and the old lady pressed her hands against her own chest. 'I just felt like you needed to know,' she said to Trinity's mom. 'She'll get herself in all sorts of trouble if she's not careful.'*

Yes, being grounded last week did ring bells.

But as an aside, victim-blame much? Sure, yes, okay, hitchhiking wasn't the ideal mode of public transport. But still, 'she'll get herself in all sorts of trouble' seemed all kinds of wrong.

'So, where were you off to this afternoon?' the mom repeated.

'I don't remember.'

'If I hear that you were heading to the Greek…' The unfinished sentence held a threat of serious consequences.

Holly frowned. 'Greek restaurant?'

'You're hilarious. No. The Greek Theatre. Sound familiar?' Again with the sarcasm.

Trinity had argued that morning, 'But they're our friends! They're helping us with our band, and we've already organised to go meet them this afternoon.'

'Trinity,' Mom said, 'I know nothing about these guys apart from that you met them at a gig. And they're so much older than you girls. It's not appropriate to hang out with them like groupies.'

Fury rose in Trinity's chest. 'You know what's not appropriate? Ruining my plans today. On my actual birthday. What about the party tomorrow night? I suppose I can't go to that either? I'm sixteen years old now. Today. It's official. You can't tell me what to do anymore.'

Yes, Holly had to admit that the Greek did sound familiar.

'No, I definitely wasn't going there,' she said. 'I wouldn't do that.' Although she wouldn't have sworn on the Bible to the fact.

'All right then. If you weren't going there, where were you going?'

'I don't know.'

'Trinity,' the mom said, sounding tired all of a sudden, 'I'm worried that I should be calling the police, but I don't even know what I'd tell them. I'm making a special dinner for your birthday, I've bought all this beautiful food that you like, but of course here we are, fighting. As per usual.'

Holly took a step backwards, like she'd been slapped. It was the 'as per usual' that did her in. Her Grannie Aileen had used the phrase on a regular basis. Not to Holly, and not usually within Holly's hearing, but Holly always knew her mum was on the other end of the phone when 'as per usual' was hissed near the end of the conversation.

'You're too busy to see your own daughter, as per usual.'

'Let me guess, Frances. Something's come up, as per usual.'

'You forgot, as per usual.'

Holly remembered trying so hard when she was growing up. To be sweet. Helpful. Easy. To get good marks at school. To be pretty. Exceptional. Perfect. Except she never got it right – or at least never got it right enough for her mum to want to hang around for more than a day or two.

Everything was too confusing, too painful and strange and incorrect and inexplicable to be put into words. And now, on top of everything, 'as per usual' – the straw that broke the camel's back. Holly burst into tears. Unstoppable, bawling sobs.

The mood in the kitchen flipped. Trinity's mom brought her in close, hugging her. 'Oh hon, I'm sorry.

I'm just worried about you, that's all…been a hard few months…just want you safe and happy…'

As the litany of soothing words continued, Holly slowly settled down. She couldn't be sure how long they stood in the kitchen, her head resting against the mom's shoulder, her arms around this stranger. At first she was clasping Trinity's mom because she needed someone to hold her steady, and then she was holding on to Trinity's mom because it felt nice. She wished her own mum had hugged her like this, maybe even once in her entire life.

She'd had Grannie Aileen, though. She'd been a big hugger. A cascade of hugs fell through Holly's memory.

The broken-collar-bone, 'you'll be fine, it's not a big operation' hug (it had been a big operation, a steel plate screwed into her bone, but the hug made her feel better).

The 'clever cookie' hug after another glowing report card.

The 'I'm here, I've got you' hug after she'd fainted. That had been a common one in her teenage years—

And then Holly remembered.

When I came out of my joint, he was trying to lift you into his car…I asked him what was going on, and he said you'd fainted…

'The guy told Lewis I'd fainted,' Holly said suddenly.

'You've been doing that a bit lately,' the mom said. 'You have to remember to eat. Have you drunk any water today?'

'I don't know,' Holly mumbled. 'I don't remember.'

The mom resumed rubbing her back, saying, 'It's okay, you're okay, everything'll be all right,' setting off a new round of tears from Holly.

As her sobs subsided again, the mom took a deep breath. 'Now why don't you go and wash your face, get ready for your special birthday dinner? My big four-year-old girl.' And she gave Holly a kiss on the forehead.

Holly smiled. The same joke must be said to every leap-year baby alive.

7.04 pm

Trinity's sixteenth-birthday dinner consisted of prawns with artificially coloured orange seafood sauce served in cut-crystal champagne glasses, beef stroganoff with rice and cooked-too-long peas, and sponge cake with pink icing. Four candles were poked into the top of the cake (that leap-year joke again) and lit with a match, to be blown out by the birthday girl herself.

Except not exactly the birthday girl herself.

Holly's head felt like it was being chiselled from the inside. Like she was about to explode from the weight of the day. The phone had kept ringing throughout dinner and Loolah kept jumping up to answer it, holding the receiver out in Holly's direction and saying, 'It's for you, it's…' [Susie Sioux, Aprilmayjune, Heather, Lewis, take your pick, someone different each time]. And in response, Holly had just kept on shaking her head because she didn't want to speak to any of them. Didn't know what she'd say.

The only person who received more than a 'she can't talk right now' was Lewis, but it wasn't Holly who spoke to him. It was the mom. Holly could hear her in the kitchen now, asking him what had happened that afternoon, but it sounded like she was getting a similar response from Lewis: *don't know, not sure, can't say exactly*.

There was so much Holly didn't know: for example, the classic, 'Why am I here?' … or, in her case, how? Although perhaps the 'why' was just as important, as surely it wasn't possible to land in a whole other person's life without there being a good reason for it? Then again, it wasn't possible to land in a whole other person's life, full stop. It just didn't happen. And yet here she was.

'Trin?' the mom said, coming back to the table. 'You've gone white as a sheet. Are you okay?'

Holly's heart was beating hard, not a racing *thump-thump-thump*, but an irregular *thumk-pthrumpth-th-rump*. She thought she might throw up.

Shifting into nurse mode, the mom put the back of her hand up to Holly's forehead. After a moment, she took her hand away, satisfied there was no fever, but clearly still concerned there was something else wrong. She looked at Holly searchingly. 'Do you feel dizzy? You're not going to vomit, are you? Maybe you hit your head this afternoon?'

Holly looked up. Concussion. The mom thought she had concussion. And actually, it made sense. Amnesia would work too. In a flash of understanding, she realised the most logical answer: none of it was real. She'd made it all up. She was a sixteen-year-old girl called Trinity, and this was her life, and it always had been. It was the only thing that made sense.

'I think I must have knocked my head when I fainted,' Holly said, half to herself, 'and I got a weird kind of...altered memories thing, something like that.

I thought I was forty years old. From Melbourne. But that's not right. I'm sixteen. Today is my birthday. My name is Trinity Byrne.'

'You thought you were forty?' Loolah asked, a giggle escaping her.

'You thought you were in Florida?' the mom said.

Holly looked from one to the other. Apart from everything else, there was a Melbourne in Florida? Who knew?

'Or are you talking about Melbourne Avenue? Around the corner?' Loolah said.

Holly wasn't sure if there really was a Melbourne Avenue around the corner, or if Loolah was making a joke.

'Who's the president?' Loolah asked, seemingly enjoying this peculiar new version of her sister.

Holly would have struggled to name the prime minister of Australia at this point. 'Boris Johnson,' she finally managed. And then she shook her head. No. He was the UK prime minister in the future. The president. America, 1980. It was…'Ronald Reagan?' she guessed.

The mom laughed uncomfortably. 'Hope not,' she said.

'No, wait,' Holly said. 'I've got this.'

Her mum had been in the kitchen, handing Grannie Aileen a bag. She was wearing a T-shirt – a souvenir from the time she'd spent in LA – with 'CARTER' printed across it in big letters, and 'MONDALE' underneath. 'I can't do this anymore. I need Holly to stay here with you for a while. It's all too hard.'

'Carter,' Holly finally said. 'Jimmy Carter. And Walter Mondale.'

'Maybe I should take you to the hospital,' the mom said.

'But Carter's right, isn't it?'

Mondale she was a little hazy on, but she was positive it was Jimmy Carter.

The mom nodded warily.

'See. I'm fine,' Holly said.

Because she was this girl, Trinity Byrne, and the alternative reality simply couldn't be.

2.14 am

Holly's eyes blinked open. She didn't know where she was, but the bed felt wrong. The pillow wasn't hers. The very darkness of the room was a different shade and texture from what she was used to. The streets outside sounded nothing like home. Her body was unable to move, in that way of deep, deep sleep. Maybe she was dreaming. It was hard to tell.

Someone was standing in the middle of the room, looking down on her. A thought filtered up through the fog of her brain. A man had been trying to put her into his car. He was dangerous. He wanted to do her harm.

The person leant towards her now. Close. Closer. And then a female voice whispered, 'Just checking. You feeling okay?'

And Holly realised that it was Trinity's mom and mumbled a vague, 'Hm,' before drifting back to sleep.

Day 2

SATURDAY,
1 MARCH
1980

8.47 am

Holly lay with her eyes firmly shut. She didn't want to open them. Didn't want to see if she was still in the strange life of a sixteen-year-old girl in Los Angeles in 1980. But she had to admit there'd be a sense of disappointment if she woke up to find herself back in her old life. Didn't want to be her old self. Didn't want to be someone new.

She turned onto her side and bunched the pillow over her head. That was the first clue, right there. Holly liked her pillow firm, but this one was soft. She lifted her arm out from under the covers and patted around, feeling the scratchiness of a woollen blanket and sheets. Not a doona. She prodded gently at the cheekbones that felt like they'd been ruled according to geometric principles. The mouth. The eyes. The browbone. The hair that she could drag her fingers through, right past her shoulders. The left ear with the run of keepers up the ridge.

There was a gentle knock at the door.

Holly considered lying doggo, but after a moment she pushed the pillow off her head and opened her eyes to an overload of yellow walls, lamp, curtains; clothes on the floor, books junked on top of the bookcase, towel still on the floor.

The mom was standing in the doorway, arms folded across her chest, leaning one hip against the doorframe. Holly recalled the sweeping sense of safety she'd experienced in the middle of the night when she'd realised it was Trinity's mom looking down at her.

'How are you feeling this morning?' the mom asked, coming over and sitting down on the bed, putting her hand against Holly's forehead, taking Holly's hand in her own.

It felt so comfortable. Of course it did. Because this was her mom, and this was her life. She had to remind herself that the whole other this-isn't-me thing wasn't real. It was concussion. Although she *also* had to admit it felt slightly awkward to be holding the hand of a woman she barely knew.

She pried her hand away and yawned expansively, mouth wide, both hands up in the air, and then plonked them back down on the bed on the left side of her body. Away from the mom.

'I'm good,' Holly said.

'You sure?'

'Yeah.'

'Not dizzy?'

'No.'

'Not feeling sick?'

'No.'

'President of the United States?'

'Carter.'

'Okay. Good. You're looking much better. You were so pale last night. Don't forget you've got lunch at Dad's today.'

The mom stood up to leave as if it was all settled – as if Holly was going to go around to some strange man's house and eat food with him.

Not that he was a stranger. It was her dad. She was just struggling to remember him at the moment. Concussion would do that.

Holly shook her head reflexively, pulling her blankets back up around her collarbone.

The mom frowned, then sat back down on the bed. 'What's the matter?'

'I don't feel well.'

'You just said you felt fine.'

'Not well enough to go for lunch.'

'It's lunch with Dad.'

'Still,' Holly said. As if that was explanation enough.

The mom was having none of it. 'Toots, Dad wants to see you for your birthday. It was hard enough for him not being here last night. For all of us. He's expecting you today.'

Holly slid her eyes away and used her baby-blue, chewed-down fingernail to pick at the corner of one of the magazine pages sticky-taped to the wall. 'I feel woozy.'

The mom steamrollered on. 'Trin, we're all managing as best we can. And it's all been arranged. Dad's looking forward to it, so's Loolah, and so were you until this morning.'

'Loolah can go on her own.'

'It's your birthday. And she can't ride all that way on her own. No, it's all organised, so scoot, up you get.'

The mom stood up without another word and left Holly in bed.

Holly couldn't pretend. This wasn't her life. None of it was. Deep down in her gut, in her soul, she knew this wasn't who she was. Holly didn't know how to behave with a dad. She hadn't grown up with one. What happened when you had a dad? What sorts of things did you talk about? What did it feel like? She'd always wanted a dad, and now she had the opportunity to have one. Except this guy wasn't hers – he was someone else's. He was Trinity's. And she wasn't Trinity.

And then all the swirling thoughts pulled sharply into focus and she couldn't escape those big questions again: what was she doing here? Why had she landed in this girl's life? Surely there was more to it than them both being leap-year babies?

Holly sat up in bed and looked around her. The orange typewriter sitting in the middle of the desk snagged her attention.

Dear Brother Orange

Two videos ran inside her head, like on a split screen. On one side was Evie giving her the typewriter at lunch yesterday. In 2020.

'It's forty. You're forty. You two were made for each other...'

Meanwhile, a different video ran on the other side of the screen:

The Christmas tree in the corner had been too small, with only a few insignificant baubles on it. The two boxes underneath had been professionally but impersonally wrapped. Mom was the one who usually wrapped their presents. Here was proof (as if it was needed) that her parents really weren't together anymore. There'd been something sad but also, admittedly, slightly thrilling and grown-up about it: her and Loolah and Dad alone, no Mom. She'd torn the paper off her present, more to get rid of the sense of some gift-wrapping stranger in the room than to see what Dad had gotten her.

'For all that poetry that's inside you,' Dad had said.

Same typewriter, different versions.

That must be the link. The birthdays weren't enough. But how? How did a typewriter have the wherewithal to plonk her into this life here?

Holly got up and padded over to the desk. She stared down at the typewriter like it was a clue and if she concentrated hard enough, it would tell all. She felt that it could sense her looking at it, as though it was waiting for her to do something.

There was the only-just-started letter from yesterday. Yesterday in 1980 *and* 2020.

Dear Brother Orange

She settled her fingers over the middle band of keys: the 'A', the 'S', the 'D', the 'F', the 'J', 'K', 'L' and the semicolon. There was a slight sensation under her fingertips, as if the keys were vibrating. If she didn't know better she'd swear there was a pulse inside the orange enamel body. A shiver ran down her spine, as if someone had pretended to crack an egg on her head then blown on the back of her neck, like they used to do in primary school. She pulled her hands abruptly away, clasping them to her chest.

She started shuffling through all the other pieces of paper scattered about the desktop. Letters. Abandoned diary entries. Poems. Bad ones.

I'm in the classroom, it's the one right
    next to you
You slip a note to me, she doesn't have
    a clue
The fact you're with her, it really makes
    me blue...

She remembered writing this, fingers on the keys, composing line by line.

They'd snuck out the back at Molly's party. Keith had put his hand over hers, even though he was with Lisa. When he'd passed her a note in the hallway at school the next day, there'd been a sense of it all being very dramatic, clandestine, doomed. Romeo and Juliet *sprang to mind. She'd come home from school that day and started typing up the poem, then yanked the sheet out when she realised she didn't feel any of it. Didn't really feel blue, only wrote that because it rhymed with 'clue' and 'you'. Truth be told, she didn't even like Keith all that much.*

Holly picked up another one.

```
Here's my neck, feel free to bite
It's early yet, we got all night
Just dip your mouth under my chin
Your teeth are sharp, it's not a sin
Now here's a scar, well lah-di-dah
You don't own me, you're not my tsar.
I'm not some victim drained and blue
The tables turned and I own you
Or maybe not, I can't tell yet
But next black night, I'll cash my debt
```

That was more like it. Genuine. Real. Her. And then the last scrap of paper in the pile.

Dear Brother Orange,
    I'm being held captive in my own home. Grounding is against my constitutional rights. The whole hitchhike grounding thing is a massive overreaction. I'm sick of Mom trying to control me! School was same old today. Boring. Learnt nothing. Hard to know what the point of it all is. Make music, not math, I say.

She remembered writing it all. Her name was Trinity Byrne and these were her words. Except, of course, she wasn't. Holly still knew deep down in her soul that she wasn't this person.

She pulled the only-just-started page out of the typewriter. Dear Brother Orange. It unsettled her. She wanted it gone. Of everything, that page with those three words was the strangest (and in the current circumstances, that was really saying something). She stuffed it into the rubbish bin, then went downstairs to look for something to eat.

She could feel this body's habit of Frosted Flakes in a bowl with cold milk every morning – but she didn't eat processed rubbish. She started her days with yoga and a couple of quick kata from karate, followed by a breakfast she concocted herself, filled with sliced almonds and pepitas and sunflower seeds and chia seeds and almond meal and dried cranberries and flaked coconut, with a small amount of milk.

Holly searched the orange-laminate pantry and found bread (white) and a jar of peanut butter. What about the whole peanut-butter-and-jelly thing that Lewis was so against? She'd never had it, but if ever a person was going to try such a thing, now was the time. She found a jar labelled 'Smucker's Grape Jelly' near the back of the pantry.

'What are you making?' Loolah called from the lounge room where, from the sound of things, she was watching morning cartoons.

'Peanut butter and jelly. Want some?' Holly yelled back.

'Yeah. Thanks.'

Holly put two slices of bread in the toaster and wondered exactly how much of each ingredient she was supposed to put on top. Did you use butter as well? And which went first, the peanut butter or the jelly? So many questions, and no smart phone to google with.

While she was waiting for the toast to pop, she picked up the newspaper lying on the bench. It was the same one she'd seen the night before. Friday, 29 February 1980.

Yesterday Holly hadn't really registered anything aside from the masthead and the date, but now she started reading, catching up on what was news in 1980. If she wasn't going to get tripped up in this stranger's life, she needed to know what was going on. A nuclear moratorium had ended. Guerillas had released thirteen people from an embassy in Colombia. Sperm donors were being awarded the Nobel Prize (seriously?).

At the bottom of the front page was the weather: mid to low seventies. Was that hot, cold or mild? Through the window it looked sunny. She remembered from yesterday afternoon that the air had felt coolish when she'd woken up on the footpath – on the *sidewalk*. If February in Australia was the end of summer, it must be the end of winter here in the northern hemisphere. She guessed it might be around about twenty degrees Celsius. Again, a smart phone wouldn't go astray here.

She started leafing through the paper. *Carter's Dilemma on Inflation* (ahem, that'd be *President* Carter). *Florida Getting Radio Moscow on AM Band*. Ads for Fred Astaire Dance Studios. The toast popped, but Holly didn't notice – she was too engrossed in 1980. There were illustrated fashion ads featuring men with their arms folded across their chests and a look as if to say, *I might be a pen-and-ink drawing, but I can still look stylish and lead board meetings*. Not to mention an entire page of cartoons – Andy Capp and the Wizard of Id and Dennis the Menace and Star Wars and BC, and that didn't even cover half of them.

She flipped over to a page featuring a column of horoscopes. Holly wasn't a horoscope reader as a general rule, but these were not general-rule circumstances. If anything was going to make you reconsider your stance on astrology and all things supernatural, it was waking up to find yourself in someone else's body forty years into the past.

Sometimes referred to as the Date of Resetting, the column read, *February 29 is thought to contain a peculiar spiritual vibration that impacts directly on time and makes time travel possible (time, of course, being the fourth dimension, and February 29 occurring once every fourth year).*

'PBJ,' Loolah called out from the lounge room. 'Waiting on my PBJ. Sometime before the end of forever would be nice.'

Holly didn't answer.

Leap days that fall at the start of each new decade are considered especially auspicious. Today's leap day has an incredibly rare spiritual frequency because it is the last Date of Resetting for the twentieth century, as well as being the last Date of Resetting for this millennium. This is a once-in-a-thousand-years date and enormous mystical events can be expected to transpire.

Loolah marched into the kitchen. 'Where's my peanut butter and jelly?' she demanded.

Holly looked over at her, eyes glazed, then pointed at the toast going cold in the toaster.

'I don't want *toast*,' Loolah said. 'You said you were making peanut butter and jelly.'

Date of Resetting. Time travel. Enormous mystical events. Once-in-a-thousand-years.

Holly wasn't sure what any of it meant, but for the first time since she'd woken up on the footpath out the front yesterday afternoon, she had a sense that if she thought about it hard and long enough, she just might be able to grasp what she was doing here.

12.04 pm

The two sisters rode their bikes down the streets of Los Feliz without helmets – in the crazy, chaotic LA traffic, young heads exposed, soft brains ready to be crushed like goo against car bonnets.

Holly had gone all through the house searching for helmets.

'Since when have we ever worn bike helmets? Do we even *own* bike helmets?' Loolah had said. Then she'd added, 'I guess if you're a forty-year-old from Melbourne you might need one,' and laughed at her own joke before hopping on her bike and riding out of the driveway without even stopping to look first.

Exactly! Holly felt like calling out to her. She'd frantically climbed onto her bike and followed the little girl out onto the street, wobbling perilously every time a car came close. Which was constantly. The two of them rode handlebar to handlebar (even though Holly kept trying to pull back, worried that side by side they presented a wider target), as Loolah discussed the plot of the *The Neverending Story*, which she was currently reading.

'…and the Childlike Empress asks him to speak her name out loud, but Bastian doesn't because he doesn't believe it's really real…'

They rode past mid-century buildings featuring blond brickwork in repeated geometric patterns; neon signs advertising drycleaners and beauty salons and barbers and Chinese restaurants; twenty-four-sheet posters announcing the latest movies: *Kramer vs Kramer, The Amityville Horror, Apocalypse Now, Alien, 10, The Muppet Movie.*

Holly took in the palm bushes and dry lawns and parched garden beds in people's front yards. 'For Rent' signs were tied to palm trees, with phone numbers to call to apply. And the cars – there were lots and lots of cars, all of them slung low on the road like hammocks, their looming bonnets coming at her unexpectedly from the left rather than her right, nearly bowling her over at each intersection.

As they rode along, Holly tried to catalogue the facts as she knew them inside her brain, but everything was slippery and confused. She knew (how, she wasn't sure – she supposed in the same way she knew everything and nothing about this girl's life…) that the dad's name was Woody. That he was tall, dark, handsome: classic movie-star looks, which made sense because he'd been an actor back in the day. His chin was slightly overlarge. Now he worked as a scriptwriter on a daytime soap called *Everingham Hospital*. That was how he'd met the mom – she'd got a job as a continuity assistant, making sure all the medical scenes were authentic, that the symptoms matched up accurately to the Disease of the Week, that the make-up gave the appropriate sickly hue to the actor. They'd fallen in love, got married, had two kids, and then, unexpectedly, he'd moved out just before Christmas.

Again Holly wondered what it was like to have a dad. How was she expected to behave? What would they do when they saw each other? Would they hug? Kiss? Shake hands? No, she knew they wouldn't shake hands. But the hug? The kiss? Who knew?

A car beeped its horn, startling her, causing her to nearly crash. Brain goo everywhere.

Holly shook her head, flinging all thoughts of the dad out onto the bitumen behind her and riding away from them.

'...and Bastian ends up in Fantasia, and the Empress gives him a note that says "Do What You Wish", but every time he makes a wish, he loses one of the memories of his life as a human, and...' Loolah was saying.

Tuning in, Holly wondered whether maybe that was going to happen to her. Would she remember less and less of her old life the longer she stayed in this world? Was there a chance of her being Bastianed? She tested her memories, poking gingerly at them like she would a bruise.

Evie and Noah and their two cutest-kids-ever, Mercy and Hope.

Thirty-two Mulroy Street, Prahran – the little house she'd bought with the money Grannie Aileen had left her in her will.

'I Am Woman' playing as they carried Zoe's coffin out.

Michael picking her up from Mulroy Street and the two of them driving down to Lorne for the weekend.

The memories ached against the surface of her skin and deep into her chest. They were real, all right. But what about this – this life she'd been thrown into? The mom. Loolah. Lewis. Her bedroom. The familiarity of it all.

The *tick-tick-tick* of the playing cards Loolah had stuck in her wheel spokes made a pleasant, soft sound as Holly fell back into single file, letting the little sister take the lead.

Loolah skidded to a stop out the front of a two-storey brick building, dumped her bike where she was standing, and ran over to buzz the buzzer. Holly's heart thumped. She didn't want to go up. She looked for a bike lock to tie the bikes together but there were none, because this was 1980 and bike locks probably hadn't been invented yet. She finally leant both their bikes against the wall out the front, wiped her palms down the front of her windcheater, then walked up the stairs.

At the top was an open front door with a brass number '4' screwed into the wall beside it. She walked in and there he was, standing in the hallway, his arms still around Loolah. The dad. Looking exactly as she knew he would.

'You took your time,' he said. 'What were you doing downstairs?'

The façade that she'd managed to keep up while she'd been riding with Loolah crumbled like a sandcastle wall. The strangeness of it all, the fact of having a dad for the first time in her life, not knowing for sure what was real and what wasn't – it was too much. She covered her face with her hands, tears streaming down her cheeks, too fragile to deal with something as simple as 'you took your time'.

The dad put his arms around her, instantly concerned. 'Wait. Hang on. I was just messing with you, kiddo.'

'She was being weird last night too,' Loolah said. 'Wouldn't speak to any of her friends on the phone…'

'You haven't had a fight with them, have you?' the dad asked into her hair.

Holly shook her head. But who knew? Maybe she had.

'…and then she said she thought she was from Melbourne,' Loolah went on.

'Melbourne, Florida?' the dad said.

'… and she fainted out the front of our place yesterday. Mom thinks she's got…um…percussion…'

'Concussion?' the dad checked.

'Yeah, I think so, and this morning she asked if I wanted peanut butter and jelly, but then she made toast instead, and she nearly got run over about seventeen times on the way here.'

'You don't make PBJ with toast,' the dad said to Holly.

'I know,' Loolah said. 'Exactly. And there was some guy, something happened with some guy.'

'What guy?' the dad asked.

Hearing the sharpness in the dad's voice, Holly realised that she hadn't given this matter enough thought. Yesterday with Lewis, she'd been occupied with trying to get things straight in her head. With the mom, she'd been busy trying to find her feet. She'd had so many other things snagging her attention since she'd woken up on the footpath yesterday, but now, here, within the safety of the dad's arms, she had to wonder what that guy *had* been doing. Was he really trying to help a girl who'd fainted as he was driving past? Or was it something more sinister? Should they be going to the police? But what would she say? She had no description to provide, no idea whether he was old, young, or in between, what colour his hair was, if he had any identifying facial features, any of the things police would traditionally ask for in these matters.

There were too many things she didn't know. And standing here with the dad's arms around her felt awkward and comforting at the same time.

'Trinity?' the dad repeated. 'What guy?'

'Nothing,' she said. 'He was no one. Just a guy trying to help out when I fainted.'

'You fainted? Again?'

Holly felt herself being overwhelmed. It was easier to keep sobbing than to answer the unanswerable questions being thrown her way. She relaxed into a full-blown crying jag, really wallowing in it, which actually felt incredibly cathartic. Finally, she started feeling settled despite herself, and the dad guided her to the couch and said, 'I've got something that will cheer you up.' He unwrapped his arms from around her and left the hallway, coming back with a gift-wrapped guitar-shaped parcel with a card sticky-taped to it.

A guitar. For the most unmusical person imaginable. This was not going to end well.

Holly read the card ('Happy 4th Birthday', of course, ha ha), then unwrapped the present and grimly flipped the heavy case open to reveal an electric guitar nestled in orange velvet. It had a smooth maple neck and two-tone body finish (a white body with a sunburst of rusted red seeping to the edges), a gold bridge, tuners and pickups: words she wouldn't normally know. The name 'Lotus' was written in a flourish at the head.

A Lotus Strat.

She put the case down at her feet, then lifted the guitar onto her knees.

'Do you like it?' the dad asked.

'It's nice,' she said, staring dumbly down at it. What the hell was she going to do with this? She didn't know her A from her middle C. Although apparently she knew her tuners from her pickups.

'I know it's not a Fender, or a Gibson,' the dad went on. Holly felt a judder of recognition – that was what Trinity had been hoping for. 'But the guy in the shop said the Lotus was just as good. Nearly as good. Better value for money. And, you know, I thought…' and he let the rest of the sentence hang in the air.

'Better value for money' equalled 'the others are bloody expensive'.

'It's beautiful,' Holly said, plucking at the strings in embarrassment. And it was – it was a really beautiful guitar. It was just that she didn't know how to play it. 'I love it. Thanks…' She couldn't bring herself to say 'Dad'. It just felt too weird inside her mouth.

'Play us something,' the dad said. He was watching her, waiting. Smiling, expectant.

She strummed the strings, trying to get a feel for the instrument. She was going to make a fool of herself. But as she started tinkering, her fingers took off with a mind, or a memory, all their own. Her body was plucking the strings, listening for tone, adjusting the tuning pegs, bringing the waist of the Lotus closer under her arm, turning the random notes into a cohesive, beautiful song drawn straight from the soul of the instrument, knowing exactly how long to hold each note, where to move her fingers on the neck. It resonated surprisingly loudly, for an electric guitar that wasn't plugged in. It had a long...her brain reached for the word...a long sustain, the chords lingering. She felt a buzz in her chest at the thought of plugging this baby in. It was going to sound spectacular.

Holly couldn't know how many hours this body had practised, or how much was bred-in-the-bone natural talent, but even listening from the inside of this body, she could hear that the Lotus was being played like a dream. The fingers were confident, feeling their way without her eyes needing to get involved, finding the exact notes without a single wrong move.

She'd never considered herself musical.

And yet, here she was.

4.23 pm

Holly and Loolah rode home, Holly balancing the heavy guitar case across her knees. You'd have thought the dad would have given them a lift. But no. He'd just waved them off.

Again, she nearly got bowled over by traffic coming unexpectedly from the left an alarming number of times, although perhaps slightly less often than on the way over. That was what you called progress, right there.

The mom was in the kitchen getting things sorted for dinner. She tsked when she saw the gift, and made some comment about it being too expensive. Something along the lines of, 'How many guitars does one girl need?' Holly looked at the mom's back and felt the hurt that was clinging to her. Woman to woman, she knew.

A wet wodge of sadness had lodged in her throat when Evie had mentioned that she and Noah had caught up with Jamie and his new girlfriend. 'I didn't expect her to be there, I'd thought it was just going to be the three of us…'

And Holly had ploughed through the wet wodge to say, 'Oh, no, no, of course, I mean, Jamie and Noah are good friends, of course you're going to be hanging out with her,' whereas what she'd wanted to say was, 'NO! You're MY friends, you should be on MY side, I DON'T WANT YOU going out and having a good time with him and his new girlfriend!'

Sometimes she wondered if the reason she'd chosen to be with Michael was because she knew he'd never be able to hurt her the way Jamie had.

Holly looked at the mom's back and wondered how it must feel to have broken up with your husband, knowing that your children were still going over to see him, spending time with him, enjoying his company. It wasn't rational to mind that, but even though the reasonable side of the mom no doubt understood it was important for her children to happily see their dad, her emotional side probably leant more towards, *'NO! I want you to be on MY side.'*

Relationships were complicated. Holly went over to the mom and gave her a woman-to-woman hug.

'A guitar's good,' she said, 'but it's not a pair of brand-new birthday Aviators.' She took the silver-framed reflective Ray-Bans from the top of her head and swung them by the arm in front of the mom.

A pleased smile briefly scudded across the mom's face before she managed to stifle it and said, 'Oh toots, I'm not in competition with your father.'

Of course she was.

The *brriing* of the phone interrupted the moment. Holly stepped back, away from the mom, away from the phone. She picked up the guitar and went to go upstairs to her bedroom, but the mom looked over at her, as if it was a foregone conclusion that Holly would pick it up.

Brriing! Insistent.

Holly wasn't ready for the outside world yet, even if it was only coming in through the phone line. The mom pursed her lips, then reached over and picked up the receiver. 'Hello? Yeah, sure hon, here she is.' And she passed the phone over to Holly. 'It's Susie Sioux.'

Holly's instinct was to hang up the phone and deal with the consequences later. But if she didn't talk to this girl, the mom would know something was up. Slowly she put the guitar back down on the kitchen floor, stalling for time, then picked up the receiver and said, voice neutral, 'Hello.'

'What's going on with you?' the girl on the other end said, her voice husky. 'Did your mom tell you I called, or what? Lewis told me some guy was trying to drag you into his car yesterday, is that really for real? He said that's why you didn't make it to the Greek. We caught up with those guys, by the way – what a waste of time that was. I hate to say your mom was right – definitely don't tell her I said that. Are you coming tonight?

Tell her you're staying at my place. Tell her we'll be home by twelve. It's not fair if she doesn't let you come.'

All said without a gap, until now, for Holly to get a word in.

Holly could feel the mom watching her, so she dragged the phone with her into the lounge room, away from prying eyes and, for that matter, prying ears. 'She's saying no,' Holly said quietly into the receiver.

'Tell her my mom's going out, and I'm scared to stay home on my own. No, wait, if she knows my mom's not home she definitely won't let you stay. Tell her my mom's going to pick us up at twelve on the dot. Promise her we won't do anything bad.'

Holly laughed. 'Pretty sure she wouldn't believe that.'

'Just *ask* her,' Susie Sioux pressed.

'She already said no.'

'Ask again.'

Holly pressed the phone against her chest, waited a good amount of time, then put the phone back to her ear. 'She's still saying no.'

'Doesn't she remember being a teenager? Maybe she never was one. My mom definitely wasn't. So what's the deal with that guy, anyway? Was he trying to put you in his car, or what? That's what Lewis said. Are you okay?'

'Yeah, I'm fine. I mean, I might have concussion, I think I fainted, Loolah keeps saying I'm acting weird' – she might as well set up alibis for the future – 'but I feel okay.'

'So who was he? Did you know him? What did he look like?'

Holly felt overcome by tiredness. She didn't want to have to rehash the thing about the guy again. She knew nothing. She didn't know the circumstances of it, who he was, or what he looked like. All she knew was that even if he *had* been trying to abduct her, he hadn't managed it. She was fine. She was here, living this life. The guy in the car was a non-starter.

'I don't know. He must have seen me faint and then pulled over to help. I don't remember.'

'Pretty freaky if he was trying to kidnap you.'

'Yeah. I don't think that was it, though.'

As Susie Sioux kept talking, despite herself, Holly felt herself settling into a familiar, easy rhythm. She had the sense she could tell this girl with the cool, deep voice anything. Well, not *anything*, of course. Not about having a head full of memories of a whole other life. Not about coming from forty years into the future. But other than that, anything.

'How was your dad? Did you go for lunch? Did he give you that guitar you were hoping for?'

Holly laughed. It sounded like Trinity was all over everything. 'Yeah.'

'A Fender Strat?'

'No. A Lotus.'

'Oh. Well, that's good too. What colour?'

As they spoke, more and more of this strange new life came into focus. Trinity and Susie Sioux and Aprilmayjune were forming an all-girl band. The guys from the Greek had said they'd help them, introduce them to people, get them some gigs.

'So what happened with those guys?' Holly asked. It felt good to be asking a question that related to this life – that proved she was who she said she was, that she knew what was going on. Even if she didn't.

'Don't even ask. Talk about dicking us around.'

'Oh.'

'But they were always going to dick us around,' Susie Sioux decided. 'Most guys don't even like the *idea* of an all-girl band, much less the reality. Doesn't matter. We don't need them. Don't need no boy band to lend us girl band a hand.'

Holly could hear the clink of plates being put down

on the table as the mom served up food. 'I've gotta go,' she said. 'Dinner's on the table.'

'Ask her one last time about tonight. Just see if she'll change her mind.'

Holly used the same trick again, holding the receiver against her chest, then getting back on and saying, 'Still no.'

'Okay. Well, she's officially ruined your life. Anyway, we'll see you tomorrow. At least that's one thing your mom can't get annoyed about. Unless she's anti us studying together. Ha ha.'

'Tomorrow?' Holly felt a bubble of anxiety rise in her stomach at the thought of the two of them sitting together studying. Talking to Susie Sioux on the phone was one thing, but seeing her in the flesh, eye to eye...?

Holly wasn't sure what they were supposed to be studying tomorrow, or where, but she could guarantee that she wasn't going to be there.

7.42 pm

Holly looked around her bedroom. It was chaos. The way this girl lived was outrageous: clothes junked everywhere, papers all over the desk, piles of books and records and other general detritus everywhere.

She needed to Kondo. Except there wasn't even such a word, because there was no such person as Marie Kondo yet. Holly wasn't going to Kondo. She was going to tidy up. Simple as that.

She picked up an album from the floor. It was Blondie, *Parallel Lines*, speaking to how she felt – parallel lives running inside her head. She pulled the record out of the sleeve and put it on the portable blue turntable that was also, unsurprisingly, on the floor. Turned it to side one. The first song was 'Hanging on the Telephone'.

While Debbie Harry sang, Holly picked up clothes and started folding or hanging. Baby-pink cigarette-leg jeans. A Godzilla T-shirt. A black dress with cut-outs at the waist. An orange singlet dress, which she put on just to see how it looked (good). She experimented with differently coloured belts, put on all the necklaces that were hanging on a hook. Looked at herself in the mirror behind the wardrobe door and had to admit that really, being so young, life didn't get much better than this. She wished she'd appreciated it more the first time around – when she was living her own sixteen-year-old life, rather than someone else's.

It had been two days now of living Trinity's life. Holly stood in the middle of the bedroom and fiddled with the bangles she'd put on. They jangled as she moved her arm up then back down.

She was struck by a thought: if she'd been thrown into this life, then where did that put Trinity?

A wave of nausea ballooned as she realised there was a very big chance that Trinity was stuck inside this body as well somehow, watching Holly's every move – lunch with the dad, playing guitar, talking to Susie Sioux on the phone, trying on her clothes, bracelets jangling – all the while screaming to get Holly's attention. Like those people who said they'd been conscious for an entire medical operation – that the anaesthetic hadn't worked properly and they were very much awake and feeling every cut of the surgeon's scalpel, listening to every word said in the operating theatre, aware of every step of the process as it was happening, but unable to alert anyone to the fact.

Was that what was happening here? Holly didn't want to know. Didn't want to think about it. But that was what cowards did, right? She couldn't ignore Trinity if she was inside this body.

Holly walked over to the mirror and stared at herself. It was a shock, again, always, to see this completely different body she was in. She stepped closer to the mirror and stared deep into her own eyes. People said the eyes were the window to the soul, so if Trinity was in there, Holly should have been able to see her. She craned closer to the mirror, as if trying to step inside the irises that stared back at her.

There was nothing. No conflict. No awakeness. Trinity wasn't here.

But it still didn't answer the question of what had happened to Trinity. Or maybe it did. Maybe Trinity *was* anaesthetised, with no clue what was going on – her soul sleeping, while Holly took over for a while.

There was a light tap at the door and the mom came in, looking around with surprise at the tidied floor, then clocking the orange singlet dress Holly had changed into. She raised an eyebrow.

'Trinity. You're not planning on going to that party tonight, are you?' she asked, crossing her arms. Readying herself for a fight.

Holly shook her head. 'No. I was just trying different things on. Seeing what they look like.' She looked down at her body. 'Testing out different belts.'

The mom looked as though she didn't believe her.

'I'm not going,' Holly repeated. 'I'm grounded, remember? Besides, you might not believe this, but I'm fine with staying home. You don't need to worry. I'm not going. I don't even want to go.'

The mom's features relaxed ever so slightly, but still held the tension of her suspicions. 'Why don't you want to go? Is everything okay?'

'Everything's fine. I'm tired. That's all.'

The mom looked around the room. 'Why's everything so neat?'

Holly laughed. 'I've been tidying up.'

'Yes, I can see that. My question is, why?'

'I can mess it up again if you'd like,' Holly teased.

The mom's face finally relaxed, her arms unfolding and dropping to her sides.

'No. Don't.' She smiled. 'It's nice to see the floor for once. Such a pretty colour, that carpet.'

Holly looked down at it. The sunniness of it. 'Yeah,' she agreed. 'It is.'

'I've been calling upstairs for ages,' the mom said, remembering why she came up in the first place, 'but you didn't answer.'

'Blondie,' Holly explained, pointing to the record player.

'Hm. I could hear. April's on the phone.' The mom turned to leave.

'Wait. No,' Holly said.

She'd been pretending all day. With the mom, with Loolah, with the dad, Susie Sioux on the phone. One more act of pretence would just about break her. The mom stopped in the doorway.

'I'm on a roll,' Holly said, pointing to her bedroom floor. 'Tell her I'll call her back tomorrow,' she added. 'Otherwise I won't finish here.'

There wasn't a mother in the world who would argue with that. Clean your bedroom or talk on the phone to a friend? The mom narrowed her eyes one last time before she nodded and left the room.

Holly finished putting away her clothes, straightened up the bookcase, then looked over at the desk – the paper, the poems, pencils, a ruler, general flotsam and jetsam. And sitting innocently in the middle of it all, Brother Orange.

She frowned, then walked over.

There was a blank sheet of paper rolled into it, ready for typing. But she was sure she hadn't put any in. A creepy feeling crawled up her spine. She definitely hadn't put more paper in. The letter with Dear Brother Orange was scrunched up in the wastebasket under the desk, thrown in there this morning.

But she must have put a new page in. She just freaking herself out, forgetting what she had and hadn't done. She needed to get a grip. Holly put her hands down, hovering them over the keys. She could feel heat rising from the black letters. Or maybe not.

Probably not.

She tore the blank page out. She was going to do an experiment. She picked up a pen and wrote on the blank page: *This page is out of the typewriter. I'm not putting another one in.*

It was proof, in case she needed it. In case tomorrow she found a new page scrolled in.

Day 3

SUNDAY,
2 MARCH
1980

10.38 am

Holly opened her eyes to mid-morning light filtering in through the window, washing over the yellow-patterned walls and furnishings. She was still here in this life. Day three. She listened out for signs of the mom and Loolah, but silence pervaded. The house was quiet. Too quiet. Eerily quiet. If she didn't know better, she'd swear she was completely alone, which wasn't an idea she wanted to consider. She wanted the mom and Loolah around to distract her. To act as buffers between her and all the strangeness. To stop her from thinking too much.

She recalled the page she'd found rolled into the typewriter last night. It unsettled her to think Brother

Orange was somehow actively involved in all this – that maybe it was magic. Although magic was such a cornball phrase. Not magic. Supernatural. All-powerful. Scary as hell.

Holly sat up and looked over at her desk where the typewriter sat. Paperless. She exhaled with relief at this one thing going right. Or, at least, going normal.

She got out of bed and walked downstairs. There was definitely no one around. On the breakfast bench was a note: *Dropping L off at Sharon's then going to work from there. See you tonight. Mom xxx.*

Holly drummed her fingers on the benchtop. What was she going to do with herself all day? The cartoon tiger stared back at her from the cereal box left out on the bench. Resistance was useless.

The silence of the house weighed down on Holly's shoulders as she wandered into the lounge room, bowl of Frosted Flakes in hand. She needed noise, activity, something to do; otherwise she might fracture. Shatter. Maybe the television would keep her mind occupied – cartoons went perfectly with a sugary breakfast on a Sunday morning. But she'd never been a big television watcher – couldn't concentrate on it. The ads always interrupted just as she was settling in, distracted her, made her lose her train of thought. Instead, she went over to the stereo, knelt down and pulled out some of the records stored beneath it. She always listened to music when she was painting on weekends, back in her real life – the music helped take her away from herself.

The Andy-Warhol-illustrated cover of *The Velvet Underground & Nico* caught her eye – the distinctive, stylised banana. She turned it over and read the track list: side one, track one, 'Sunday Morning'. And today was Sunday. In the morning. She pulled the vinyl out of its sleeve and placed it on the turntable, gingerly laying the needle on the edge of the record. The bell-like sweetness of an instrument that Holly couldn't quite put her finger on, like a harpsichord but more angelic, came tinkling out of the speakers. She sat cross-legged on the floor with her bowl of cereal and listened to Lou Reed singing about Sunday morning, settling into the strangely optimistic feeling it gave her. The record spun on and next came the jangly, garage punk sound of 'I'm Waiting for the Man', followed by the distinctly lo-fi 'Femme Fatale' and the Turkish-inspired 'Venus Furs'.

As she listened to the Velvet Underground, she continued sifting through albums. Coming across the self-titled album by the Runaways, she pulled it out and had a read of the back cover. Track one was 'Cherry Bomb'. She made a quick swap of the vinyls, and soon the thumping guitar riff and the unexpectedly deep voice of Cherie Currie filled the room. It was a song that Holly knew deep down inside her core. She turned the volume up. She was home alone, and she could do what she wanted.

She stood up and started dancing around the lounge room, shoulders back, arms flung wide, enjoying the freedom of this body. She put on the Rolling Stones, 'Sympathy for the Devil', volume cranked right up, followed by the steel-stringed clang of Fleetwood Mac's 'Rumours', then the punk energy of the Ramones, her body responding to the colossal cool of these albums. She was fizzing like sherbet. She could dance for hours, run for miles. Gravity was no barrier. She felt boundless. The music filled her as she whipped her head around and jumped up and down, just like the person dancing up a storm alongside her.

Holly stopped. Stared. Wait. There was another girl here in the lounge room with her.

It was Zoe. Her best friend, alive, healthy, a teenager again, here. Holly ran over and hugged Zoe in close. The ecstacy: Zoe robust, not a skerrick of cancer, alive, alive, alive!

But as they hugged, Holly realised it wasn't Zoe at all. This girl was smaller, shorter: her body felt different. Heart plunging, Holly stepped back to look at the girl, who'd resumed dancing like an untamed animal, a grin of pure joy on her face.

It was Susie Sioux. In the flesh. Her black hair was teased to within an inch of its life. Her eyes were smudged with thick black eyeliner. Red lipstick framed the words as she sang along to 'Blitzkrieg Bop'. She wore a short denim skirt, canvas tennis shoes and a faded yellow T-shirt with 'Culture' printed across the front of it. In fact, apart from the dark hair, she looked nothing like Zoe. But her energy was the same. Susie Sioux was like a mirror of Zoe's soul.

Holly took the needle off the record and returned to gazing at this girl. Did it mean something, this synergy of a similarly energied friend: she and Trinity, aligned in another unexpected way?

'My girl!' Susie Sioux said, jumping over and hugging Holly to her again. 'We missed you last night. It was a dud party. How was your night?' She reached into her bag and pulled out a cigarette pack, fished out a slim white cylinder and jammed it into her mouth. Took a lighter out of her bag, dragged the tip of the cigarette through the flame, breathed in deeply, then offered up the pack of cancer sticks to Holly.

After everything with Zoe.

Holly pushed the pack away from her face. 'No. Yuk.'

Susie Sioux took another long drag and folded her arms across her stomach as she examined Holly. 'Who are you and what have you done with my friend?' she asked, her head tilted to one side.

Holly looked at her again, this girl who could be Zoe. It felt so good to see her, to be in the same room as her and feel her alive, vital. The true friendship of these two girls was undeniable. But there was something else going on that Holly hadn't been expecting – a physical yearning at the smell of Susie Sioux's cigarette. She ached to take one from the pack. Trinity was a smoker. But she couldn't. Not after Zoe's cancer. Holly waved the smoke away from her face, making a point that she didn't want anything to do with it.

The strangeness of the moment was not lost on Susie Sioux. 'What's going on?' she asked, narrowing her eyes.

'It's just that...' *My best friend Zoe died of cancer, and cigarettes'll kill you, just like they did her, and don't you know the damage each cigarette does to your lungs?* Obviously the truth wasn't going to cut it. '...I still feel a bit queasy from, you know, fainting out the front on Friday afternoon.'

Zoe blew a plume of smoke out the side of her mouth, away from Holly.

'Oh, yeah. That guy. But otherwise you're okay?' she checked.

Holly nodded. It was so odd, this girl just appearing in the lounge room so unexpectedly. Holly went to say, *What are you doing here?* but then she remembered the phone call from last night. Susie Sioux had said something like, *See you tomorrow, unless your mom's anti-study, ha ha.*

The two of them stood there in silence for a moment, Holly suddenly feeling the natural shyness that came with standing in a room alone with a complete stranger. Then she said, 'I should go and grab my books,' impressing herself with her ability to think on her feet. 'For us to study,' she added.

Any excuse to leave the room and compose herself.

Susie Sioux blinked at her and slowly blew out another plume of smoke. 'Okay, seriously. What are you talking about?'

'You know. You said on the phone we were going to study today.'

Susie Sioux's gaze solidified into a long stare.

Silence.

Then she let out a shout of laughter. 'Ha! Good one. For a minute there I thought maybe your head injury was more serious than anyone suspected.'

'Boo!' Two hands clapped onto Holly's shoulders from behind. Startled, she turned to face a girl with shaggy, softly curling blonde hair, eyes heavily lined in black.

April. Aprilmayjune. Another friend with a lifetime of shared memories.

Water-balloon races down the driveway at April's house. The enormous fig tree in her front yard, the three of them sitting on their favourite branch for hours talking.

'Have you been ignoring me?' April said, putting her hands on her hips and pouting.

'No. What do you mean?' Holly said. Then again, maybe she had been. Who knew?

'You haven't returned any of my calls. You're lucky I came today. I nearly wasn't going to. But' – theatrical sigh – 'you know, when a séance is on offer, who am I to refuse?'

Holly looked from Aprilmayjune back to where Susie Sioux was now crouched on the floor pulling a wooden board out of her bag. She held it up for them to see in a ta-dah moment. 'Ouija' was written along the top, with 'Yes' on the left, 'No' on the right. The letters of the alphabet were ranged across the middle like a rainbow, numbers '1 2 3 4 5 6 7 8 9 0' ran underneath that, and the word 'Goodbye' signed off at the base.

A chill ran through Holly. Everything was surreal enough – she didn't need spirits from another dimension trying to speak to her. She was struggling with how to respond to real live flesh-and-blood people.

Holly turned from Susie Sioux back to Aprilmayjune, who was watching her carefully.

'Something's different about you,' April decided, frowning.

Holly shifted her eyes away, feeling crushed on both sides. Susie Sioux knew something was up because she wasn't smoking. Aprilmayjune could sense her fakeness. Holly had known she couldn't maintain the façade for long. There were too many things to get wrong. Subtle differences, nuances.

'It's your hair,' April finally announced.

'She's not wearing eyeliner either,' added Susie Sioux.

'Gawd, I don't think I've ever seen you without eyeliner. Not since junior high. Who are you and what have you done with…' April said, not even bothering to finish the phrase.

And Holly had to laugh, because, yes, right, exactly. Who was she? And what had she done with…?

1.17 pm

Holly's bedroom was quiet and dark. The door was shut, the curtains were closed, and there was the sense that the entire room was sucking in its breath. The three girls were sitting cross-legged on the floor around the ouija board.

'Your room's very clean,' April whispered.

'If the spirits don't scare us, the cleanliness of your room is guaranteed to,' Susie Sioux said.

Holly felt the thud of a headache slowly building, like she'd been awake for days and could no longer think straight. The incense burning on the edge of the bedside table, which Susie Sioux had lit 'for mood purposes', wasn't helping.

'Okay, fingers on,' Susie Sioux said, putting her pinky on the planchette that she'd placed in the centre of the board, then nodding across at Holly and Aprilmayjune to do the same.

A ripple travelled down Holly's back, as though cold liquid was filling up her spinal column.

'This is a mistake,' she muttered. 'We shouldn't be doing this.'

Aprilmayjune winked open an eye and grinned over at Holly. 'I know, how cool is it,' she said, then shut her eye again.

'And now,' Susie Sioux whispered, getting into the zone, her hair merging with the gloom of the curtained room, her fringe casting shadows over her eyes, 'I summon the spirits of this house…'

No, Holly wanted to say. *Don't summon them. We don't want them here. Spirits, don't come. You're not welcome.*

'I call for a groundswell of the cosmic energy – a convergence of supernatural beings to answer our questions…'

No groundswell. No convergence. We have no questions for you. Holly wanted this train to stop before it got wrecked.

Sensing her discomfort, Aprilmayjune slid her gaze in Holly's direction before closing her eyes again.

Susie Sioux continued talking, her intonation mesmerising. 'We ask you to cross over into this world of the living,' she whispered. 'Speak to us. We are ready to hear from you.'

Holly felt a draught at her back, like the door had been opened. She turned around to check. It hadn't been. They'd all felt it. The three girls looked up at each other.

'Are you here?' Susie Sioux asked.

The planchette moved slowly to the top left corner.

'Yes.'

Holly breathed out, a long deep breath, reminding herself that séances weren't real. They were hoaxes. Rubbish. She just had to go along with it. This was a lark. Not to be taken seriously. Schoolgirls couldn't call spirits to them with a ouija board and planchette.

'What's your name?' Susie Sioux asked.

I don't believe in you, Holly thought. *You're not real, this is a game, ghosts aren't true, you aren't here in my house, in my bedroom, in my head. Goodbye.*

The planchette started moving to the bottom of the board. Towards *goodbye*. Holly watched it sliding down the board with a mix of horror and relief. If it could hear her inside her head, maybe she could simply wish it away.

'No, wait,' Susie Sioux said. 'Don't go. We have questions to ask. You don't have to tell us your name if you don't want to. We invited you here. We want to talk. Please stay. Do you have a message for any of us?'

Holly repeated to herself, inside her head, *Go away, go away, go away*. If the spirit was real, if it could hear her, it would get the message.

But the spirit was ignoring her, responding to Susie Sioux instead. The planchette started moving across to the 'H'. It stopped there a moment. Then backwards, to the letter 'E'. Then across to 'L'. Over to the 'P'.

'HELP.'

Then nothing.

'Oooh,' April said. 'Scary.' Her eyes were wide, her mouth grinning.

Susie Sioux looked from Aprilmayjune to Holly, thrilled that her séance was off to such a dramatic start. 'Help? Who's in danger?' she asked. 'Which one of us?'

The planchette started moving again. 'T'. Back a couple of letters to 'R'. Back further to 'I'. Forward to 'N'. Around to 'I', 'T', 'Y'.

April and Susie Sioux flicked their eyes over at Holly, whose cheeks were burning, as if caught out in a lie. And then the planchette started moving again. Faster this time. 'H'. Then 'O'. Back to 'L'. Stop.

Around the board, then doubling back to the 'L' again. Forward to 'Y'.

'Holly?' Susie Sioux asked. 'Who's Holly? Do we know a Holly?' She looked straight at Holly.

Holly shook her head, traitor that she was.

'Or maybe it's a holly bush?' April suggested. 'Maybe you need to be careful of a holly bush?'

And then the planchette moved towards the edge of the board, the tip pointing straight at Holly, accusing her. *She's a fraud! She's not who she says she is! This is Holly, here! This one!*

Holly felt as if extra weights had been slipped onto the ends of a psychic barbell she'd been trying to keep above her head ever since she'd woken up here. Her muscles were turning to flimsy ribbons. There wasn't enough air in the room, her heart was pounding, her psyche was being crushed. She wanted to stand up, toss the board away from her, leave her bedroom, but she was paralysed, unable. She wanted to at least take her finger off the planchette, to stop participating, to turn her mind blank, to not listen, to not see the words. But it was impossible. *HELP TRINITY HOLLY* was seared into her brain.

From behind them, a harsh metallic clattering sound came from the typewriter, from Brother Orange, as if a ghostly secretary was typing out a letter, a couple of quick words. Then, just as abruptly, it stopped, so quickly that it was hard to know if it had happened or not.

All three girls let go of the planchette and squealed. Holly leapt away from the board, jumping up and flinging open the bedroom door. She pushed open the curtains to let in the daylight. To get rid of the ouija madness. Susie Sioux and April were both still on the floor, looking terrified but also laughing at the craziness of it all. A possessed typewriter. Séances didn't get much better than this. Or much worse, depending on your perspective.

Holly went over to the desk to see what was written on the typewriter. But, of course, there was nothing there, because there wasn't any paper scrolled in. And anyway, typewriters didn't type randomly without someone to operate the keys. Except as she stared down at it, she noticed two black words registering faintly against the black rubber of the roller. Fuck off!

An involuntary prickle crawled through her hairline like nits.

'Did that just happen?' April said. 'Did the typewriter just type on its own? Seriously. I heard it typing on its own.'

'That was the best séance ever,' Susie Sioux said. 'I can't believe that happened.'

'But what does it mean?' April said, looking to Susie Sioux for answers – *it's your ouija board, you should know what's going on.* 'And why was it saying you need help?' she added, turning to look at Holly. 'Or is it some person you know called Holly who needs help? I'm confused. That was so awesome.'

Holly stared at the typewriter, focused on bringing her heart rate down, not wanting to look up and face these girls she'd never met until a couple of hours ago. It was all too much. She felt a pulsing pressure in her ears, an intense feeling of vertigo, a huge desire to vomit, the struggle of keeping the dead weight of her body upright.

'Trin,' Susie Sioux said. 'You okay?'

Holly nodded. Just.

'Do you know a Holly?'

She shook her head.

HELP TRINITY HOLLY.

Fraud.

5.13 pm

April and Susie Sioux had left not long after the séance, after Holly said she was feeling dizzy and strange. Holly had immediately climbed into bed, pulled the blankets over her head and fallen into the sleep of the truly overwhelmed. When she woke up, dusk was starting to deepen in the sky and everything came rushing back. She lay there trying to keep her mind a blank, but her brain was filled to bursting.

She shifted so that she was lying on her side, facing the desk.

Brother Orange. It was impossible that the typewriter had typed on its own. It couldn't have. But what else could explain what all three of them had heard? She pushed the blankets off, swung her legs out of bed and padded over to the desk. The ghostly imprint was still there on the roller. Fuck off! She felt sick just looking at it.

The typewriter was the common denominator. It was here, and it was in the future (her past, if that really was the future). The answer had to be locked inside that orange enamel body. It had called to her during the séance, asking her to come sit with it. It made as much sense as anything else that had happened these past few days. She didn't want to, but she had no choice. She had to know what was going on, and she felt that the typewriter had the answer. She rolled a sheet of paper into the body of the typewriter and waited.

Nothing. Silence.

Holly scratched at her neck, then pushed her hair off her face. It was impossible. Typewriters didn't type *to* you, you typed *into* them. It was a law of physics.

(Other laws of physics dictated that people didn't leave their bodies and end up in someone else's life, so clearly you couldn't always rely on physics.)

She wondered whether she had to type something to get it going. Maybe a few sentences about how she was feeling would trigger it – whatever *it* was. Standing over the desk, she positioned her fingers on the keys. Pulling them back, she pressed her palms together as though in prayer, then she leant forward, put her fingers back down on the keys and started typing:

What

She was going to type, *What do you want from me*, something along those lines, but before she could get it out, black letters started hammering up onto the page. The words slammed of their own volition onto the pristine white paper, the sound like a volley of bullets ricocheting from her bedroom walls.

Holly leapt away from the desk, as far away as she could get, her back huddled against the wardrobe. It was, frankly, terrifying. The séance typing had been one thing – the three of them hadn't even been sure it had happened. But this was, without a doubt, a fully fledged possession.

And then, just as suddenly as it had started, it stopped. Holly didn't move, not wanting to break the silence. When she'd worked up the courage, she slowly made her way back over to the desk, ready to scramble if the keys started up again, and looked down at the page.

What the fuck is going on? I ran out onto the street just before and some guy just told me I'm in Melbourne. In AUSTRALIA! IN 2020! But that's not the worst of it. Not even close. Melbourne, Australia in 2020 would be chicken shit compared to everything else that's going on. I'm not me, I'm some old lady with bad hair and terrible clothes. I'm not me. And no matter what I do, I can't get back to being me. I've done everything. I've chopped off all the hair ripped up all the clothes tipped the house upside down and I'm still this old person. I don't know how you did it, but it has to be your fault, because you're the only thing I recognise in this whole helltown house. What am I doing here PUT ME BACK! Just put me back or I'm gonna chop you to bits, I'll rip every single key off your keyboard and you'll NEVER be able to DESTROY anyone else's life ever again. Just CHANGE ME BACK you FUCKINBGasdfkljdlfkjs dlfkjsdazfcxvlaerhi'yoagjio;ijoajlijlagejlag erjklaasdjlkadsfasdflijadfjklzjlzjkljkljlkrefsla egriouaehtasdfajkoeiaeourtzndfgka;ertioaeior; gjagjslagleijagrjldkasdjlkadgfj;iadfo;iadguio garaiouaegriouagrehiougareijogarlbfdzlmkaj dwaeiafdmaeoitaegrjaefiawemdfjcviou aekwt4ip3q3jkk;ldfspi,ldcoawemdjcvmew aodmwepcoiwadopaweidlafksaheoaew adzkowroiOKAAEPDadsjlkaeoiuawejlkdfsoi

And that spread down the rest of the page, right through to the end.

Holly's best guess was that the gobbledygook was due to Trinity pounding her fists up and down against the keys in anger and frustration – trying, through sheer force of her fury, to change the way things were.

Holly stared at the words, feeling the confusion and turmoil and rage that was steaming off the page from Trinity's side of the…what? Typewriter? World? Universe? Up until this moment, the sum total of Holly's assessment had been that she'd somehow woken up in Trinity's body, and Trinity's soul was asleep while her body was taken over. But judging from this letter, Trinity had been flung, at the same moment, into Holly's life, forty years into the future. And it seemed fair to say that Trinity wasn't happy about it.

Holly couldn't even begin to imagine how a sixteen-year-old girl would go about processing all this surrealness. She worried that Trinity might hurt herself while she was pushing back against the situation. And let's be honest – it wasn't Holly being selfless when she worried about Trinity hurting herself. Trinity hurting herself would actually mean hurting Holly – not something she wanted to have happen. Also, what was all that about chopping off her hair? Ditto the ripping-up of her clothes?

Holly needed to calm the situation down. She took out a fresh piece of paper. She wasn't sure if this would work, but it was worth a try.

Dear Trinity, she typed.

It's me. Holly. The person whose life you've woken up in. That bad hair? It's mine.

She had been aiming for light-hearted, but maybe now wasn't the time.

I'm kidding. I mean, I'm not kidding. It's really me. Don't freak out. It sounds like we've swapped lives. I woke up out the front of your place on Friday afternoon – your birthday. 29 Feb. And I'm guessing that you woke up in my house on Saturday afternoon – my birthday. Also 29 Feb.

She wondered how much she should say.

Obviously the whole thing is weird and makes no sense, but don't panic! We're going to sort this out together, I promise. No need to tear clothes or cut hair or wreck things. Please. Best I can figure, the typewriter has something to do with it, and it looks like you've worked that out too. I think it's something to do with the fact that we're both leap-year babies. Apparently 29 February is also called the Date of Resetting, when time travel is possible. And 29 Feb 1980, your birthday, was especially powerful because it's the last leap day of the century AND millennium, so I think what's happened is your birthday fell on a kind of once-in-a-thousand-years, turbo-charged, super-powerful Date of

Resetting. Somehow, we've both been caught up in some once-in-a-thousand-years soul swap.

We held a seance today: me and Susie Sioux and April. The ouija board spelt out HELP TRINITY HOLLY. If you put a comma in there, it says: HELP TRINITY, HOLLY. I think I'm here to fix something in your life. Does that make sense?

Anyway, if you get this letter, write back. We can figure it out together. But don't do anything you might regret. Or, more accurately, that I might regret! I don't want to come back and find my life has been trashed. Ha ha.

The mom called up the stairs that dinner was on the table.

I have to go. I hope you're okay. Write back asap. Love...

She wondered if 'love' was a little too familiar – if 'from' would have been better – but once a thing is typed on an old typewriter, it's there for good, no delete, no backspace, no autocorrect. So she left it, and signed off.

Holly

Day 4

MONDAY, 3 MARCH 1980

6.48 am

School. The word nudged Holly awake. She had to get up for work. She had classes to teach, kids to wrangle, art folios to assess. She rolled onto her side and opened her eyes.

Yellow sunflowers, orangey tulips, red flowers. The LED display on the wood-grain digital clock announced the time in jumbo-sized numbers: 6.49.

She didn't work at a school; she was a sixteen-year-old student there.

'Trinity! Did you hear me?' she heard the mom calling up the stairs. 'You've got school.'

'I heard you,' Holly called back.

Obviously she wasn't leaving the house. The world outside was dangerous. If she went to school there'd be traps, their saw-toothed jaws rusted open, waiting for her to set foot into them. All of Trinity's friends would be watching her. There were too many ways to trip up. Also, there was the whole complication of which classroom she was supposed to be in when. Where her locker was. Where the toilets were. No. She was going to stay in this house, close to Brother Orange, and wait for a reply from Trinity. They needed to work out how to swap back. She wanted her old life. Bad hair and all.

She'd tell the mom she was sick again, that she had concussion, that she didn't know who the president was. Whatever she needed to say to make sure she stayed home. But then the mom called up the stairs, 'We're going. I'm dropping Lools off at early-morning practice. We'll see you tonight,' and the front door closed.

Holly smiled to herself. No need for an excuse.

She pushed off the blankets and walked over to the desk, sat down and stared at the page in the typewriter, willing it to have some kind of reply on it. It was totally blank. *Come on, Trinity, answer.*

What was going on back in Melbourne, all those years into the future? Had anyone noticed that she seemed different? It was probably Tuesday there by now, so she'd have missed the staff meeting and her meeting with Kristen about the Year 11 folios. And had Michael come back from his golfing long weekend yet? Had he come over with a present for her birthday? Not wanting to be mercenary, but she was expecting something good. Maybe he'd organised that special dinner he had promised.

And then Holly had an awful realisation. If Michael went around to her place, he'd expect that they'd tumble into bed at some stage. It was only reasonable. That was what they did – they were grown adults. But Trinity was only sixteen. Panic swelled in Holly's stomach. Michael couldn't come around. He couldn't put his hands on Trinity. It was all kinds of wrong. She wasn't even sure what the term for it would be, but it was bound to be illegal in all jurisdictions.

The typewriter did nothing. Holly finally started typing, impatient.

Did you get my letter? I need you to write back to me.

Stone-cold silence. Waiting for Trinity's reply was anxiety-making. Holly pushed her chair away from the desk and walked out of the bedroom, heading towards the bathroom. A shower would help. She washed her hair, tried to scrub all thoughts of Michael and Trinity out of her brain, avoiding looking at this body in order to give Trinity some privacy.

The hot water felt good on her skin, but the water pressure wasn't the same as home. The shampoo was fruity and smelt like chemicals, and the shower curtain glommed to her legs in a clammy way. No, even in the shower with her eyes shut tight as water ran down her face, she was keenly aware that this wasn't her life.

She towelled herself off, not looking in the mirror, then went back into her bedroom (not her bedroom), put on a dressing-gown (not her dressing-gown), and went downstairs to have some breakfast. The *LA Times* was folded up on the breakfast bench, exactly as it was every morning. Today's front-page headline read, *Body of Kidnaped Girl Found*.

As dramatic as the headline was, it was the spelling that initially struck her. 'Kidnaped' should have a double 'p'. K-i-d-n-a-pp-e-d. Holly wondered how such an obvious spelling mistake could have ended up on the front page of a major newspaper. And then she remembered. Here it was 'color' instead of 'colour', 'apologize' instead of 'apologise'; inches and feet, miles, degrees Fahrenheit.

Holly unfolded the newspaper and started reading about the girl who'd been kidnaped with a single 'p'. She'd gone missing from Atwater Village a few weeks back. Her body had been found yesterday in the Forest Lawn area near Adams Hill. Another suspected victim of the Mariposa Murderer.

Lying on the nature strip outside, staring up at the sky. 'Trinity? You okay? There was a guy. He was trying to lift you into his car.'

Was it the Mariposa Murderer? The guy who'd stopped to pick her up? Maybe she'd been wrong to discount that guy, to consider that he'd simply been helping a girl he'd seen faint as he was driving past. But then again, what were the chances of it being the same guy? She wasn't even sure where Mariposa was. Or Forest Lawn, for that matter. It could be all the way across the other side of the vast sprawl of LA, far from Los Feliz.

Had Trinity fainted, or had she been hitchhiking? Was he a good guy or bad? Then she had a chilling thought: was that why they'd swapped places? To save Trinity from him? Did she need to go to the police about this?

Holly went back upstairs to ask Trinity, to find out exactly what had happened the afternoon they'd swapped.

She was sitting down at the typewriter, fingers at the ready, when she heard something downstairs. Someone was sliding the back door open.

She looked out her bedroom window to the driveway. The car wasn't there. The mom hadn't come back for something she'd forgotten. The back door slid shut. There was definitely someone in the house. Whoever it was, they were moving around downstairs. Adrenaline flooded her body.

Body of Kidnaped Girl Found. The Mariposa Murderer. *HELP TRINITY, HOLLY.*

Lewis standing over her, asking if she was all right. 'I asked him what was going on, and he said you'd fainted and he was going to drive you home. But I pointed to your house' – all the little ducks lining up in a row, realisation bobbing – *'and said, "Except she lives there."'*

Lewis had pointed out to the guy exactly which one was her house. The one she was standing in, right now. And now the same guy had snuck in through the back door and was downstairs somewhere, looking for her.

Holly had done enough karate in her life to know that a girl Trinity's size didn't have the bulk to beat a grown man. And then she realised this was her advantage – the man wouldn't be expecting a black belt on the offensive. He'd be expecting a girl who'd maybe scream, maybe put up a bit of a fight, but not a true competitor. Even if this body had never done a lick of karate in its life, it had youth and agility on its side, while Holly had the knowledge in her head. Holly could think through the moves, and Trinity could stitch this guy right up.

Holly moved quietly down the stairs, alert for any sound. There was a scraping noise in the kitchen. He hadn't seen her yet. Her way was clear to the front door. She could simply bolt. She moved towards it, but then she stopped. This guy knew where she lived. If he wanted to get her, he'd simply come back later. Or maybe he'd come back when Loolah was home alone. No, this had to end now. That was what Holly was here for.

Help Trinity, Holly.

She crept towards the kitchen doorway and peeked around it. The guy was standing at the kitchen bench, his back to her. She could see a bag on the bench beside him. She took a deep breath, whispered, 'Yoi,' to herself (which meant 'steel yourself, get your stance right, be prepared') then slipped forward, pure karate focus, and hooked her foot in front of his ankle, yanking his leg towards her and pulling him off balance.

The guy threw out his arms and yelled. A bowl flew through the air as he fell. Frosted Flakes and milk splattered every surface.

Lewis looked up at her from the floor. 'What the fuck,' he said.

Holly blinked at him, and then relief flooded her, mixing with adrenaline and bursting out of her in a hooting kind of laughter. Of course, she should have known. Even from the back – the slim build, the clothes, even the ankles were familiar to her.

'Oh,' she said, struggling to control her giggles. 'Morning.'

He looked around at the mess she'd made, then shook his head and grinned. 'Mate,' he said, 'you should have just told me you wanted the last of the Frosted Flakes. I'd have been happy to take the Buc Wheats.'

'I'm sorry,' she said. 'I don't know why I did that. I think I've been a bit on edge ever since that guy, you know, out the front. I thought you were him.'

Lewis looked at her, all joking put to the side as concern washed over his features. 'You okay?' he asked. 'You starting to remember it?'

'Bits and pieces. Not much.' She grabbed a tea towel and started wiping down the cupboard fronts, which only served to smear milk and cereal further. 'I was worried that he'd come back to get me,' she said, sitting back on her heels and looking over at Lewis. 'I mean, seeing as he knows where I live.'

'How would he know that? For all he knows, you were walking along a random street. He couldn't possibly know this is where you live.'

Holly blinked at him. He didn't remember.

Lewis pointing to her house. Telling the guy, 'She lives there.'

Some things were obviously clearer for her from Friday afternoon, the strangeness of it imprinting every detail into her brain, whereas Lewis had been distracted, worried about her. He remembered the overview but not the minutiae. Then again, maybe she was wrong. Maybe she was the one misremembering. Maybe he hadn't pointed to her house and said, 'She lives there.'

'Do you remember what sort of car he was driving?' she asked.

Lewis shrugged. 'An American car. White. Like every other American car on the road over here.'

She knew what he meant. They all looked exactly the same to her too. Riding her bike to the dad's house, it had just been long, boaty 1970s American car after long, boaty 1970s American car.

'What did he look like?' she asked.

Lewis frowned. 'He had his cap pulled right down. And then he just dumped you and split, and, yeah, I should have taken his numberplate or something, but I didn't even think of it. I was making sure you were okay.'

'You know, I'm sure it was nothing,' Holly decided. 'Obviously I fainted, he stopped to help, and then he figured he didn't need to worry once you came over. Anyway, I think I'm only succeeding in smearing the milk even further.' She just wanted to move on from the Mariposa Murderer. Which, of course, the guy probably wasn't. 'This calls for some heavy-duty mop action.' She went and grabbed the mop from the laundry, then came back into the kitchen only to find Lewis hunched down cleaning up where she'd left off. 'Stand back,' she said, nudging him with the mop. 'Let the expert take over.'

After cleaning up and a bowl of Buc Wheats each, Lewis put his dishes in the kitchen sink and said, 'Okay, let's make tracks, we gotta get to school.'

Holly reactively shook her head. 'Oh. No. I'm not going.'

Lewis laughed. 'Yeah, right. Come on.'

'No, seriously,' Holly said. 'I don't feel good. I'm dizzy. I think I've still got concussion. From the other day.'

'Trin,' Lewis said firmly, 'you can't keep cutting school. Your mom's paying me in premium cereal to come here each morning and drag you out. So, yeah, go get ready, I don't wanna be late.'

7.28 am

Holly stood upstairs in the bathroom and looked at her face. Not her face. Trinity's. She didn't know how to do this make-up. Or this hair. She tried to remember how she'd looked when she'd first stood in front of the mirror on Friday afternoon: black eyeliner, messy hair. April and Susie Sioux had both clocked how strange she'd looked yesterday with her hair brushed and eyes unblackened.

'Hurry up!' Lewis called up the stairs.

She rustled around in a drawer and found some hair gel, but changed her mind. She was going to be in a stressful environment – she had to feel comfortable. She made an executive decision to pull the hair back up into a simple ponytail, the way she wore it most days when she was teaching. Taking out an eyeliner pencil, she ran it lightly along her top eyelashes and added some mascara. Stepping back, she took one last look at herself.

She was wearing a short denim skirt and a T-shirt with Godzilla printed on the front of it. A nylon Pan Am satchel holding her schoolbooks was slung over her shoulder and a jumper was tied around her waist in case she got cold. Her hair was glossy in its high ponytail. Her face looked fresh.

But it wasn't her. At least, it wasn't Trinity.

Holly pulled the hair tie out, took the gel from the drawer and ran a large blob of it through her hair. She ran the eyeliner under the eyelashes and across the top of her lid, taking it up towards her eyebrow, giving herself an overblown punk look.

And there she was. Trinity from Friday afternoon.

Resistance was useless.

And that'd be a sweater tied around her waist. Not a jumper. A sweater.

7.56 am

There were certain places in the world that Holly would always recognise, whether she'd been there or not: the Eiffel Tower, the Golden Gate Bridge, Sydney

Opera House, the Chrysler Building. Also, John Marshall High: the iconic American school that had featured in movies like *Bachelor Party*, *Nightmare on Elm Street*, *Pretty in Pink* and *Grease*, among others.

John Marshall High towered over Holly in a memory-expanding way. The brickwork, the sprawling lawns, the leafy trees, even the yellow school bus parked out the front – she knew this place. She spent more time here per week than she did at home.

She and Lewis joined the flow of students walking through the front doors. Inside, the corridors, lockers, noticeboards, stairwells – they were all familiar.

There were students dressed casually in T-shirts and denim. Girls in Peter Pan-collared floral shirts and floral skirts. Boys in chinos and button-down collars. Couldn't-give-a-shit girls in overalls with singlets. Surfer chicks in baggy windcheaters. Boys in checked shirts. Perfect girls with flicked-back Charlie's Angels hair. Shy boys who wore their hair over their eyes. Messy girls with hair like Trinity's. Fresh-faced girls with pale make-up and pink lipstick. It was a real mix.

So different from the students at the school where Holly taught, dressed in their identical blue uniforms, with identical blue ribbons in their hair.

She looked around and realised Lewis had gone in a different direction, but it didn't matter. The locker-lined corridors were familiar. Her feet knew the way. She stopped instinctively at her locker, opened the padlock without even having to think. 0229. Second month, twenty-ninth day. Her birthday.

It was only as she clicked the lock and opened the locker door that she realised in Australia she would have the code plugged in as 2902. Twenty-ninth day, second month.

She jammed the Pan Am satchel into her locker and took out her maths book. (Math, Monday morning first thing. She knew this as surely as if it had been written on the timetable taped to the inside of her locker. Which it wasn't. The timetable was taped there all right, but it was blank.) Then she looked around her at the people walking past. They were people whose names she knew – people whose parties she'd been at, whose cars she'd driven in.

She saw Molly and Katie, their books bundled up in their arms.

Molly in a Wonder Woman costume running past her and Susie Sioux, cradling a Halloween goblin that she'd nicked out of someone's front garden as a dare. 'Oh my god, run! They totally saw me take this!'

Ash and Daniel.

Ash driving them to Santa Monica in his mom's car, his surfboard squished between her and April in the back, Susie Sioux riding shotgun up the front.

Carl. The strangeness of his freshly shorn hair.

'Turns out, the thing I really liked about him was his curls,' April had said. 'I mean, you can't break up with someone because they've had a bad haircut. Can you?' The jury of Susie Sioux, April, Heather and Trinity had been evenly divided on whether it was a legit break-up excuse or not.

There was Scott, leaning against the wall talking to Jennifer, who'd just broken up with Kevin. Amy, who couldn't be trusted with a secret. Jess, who couldn't be trusted with a boyfriend (her own, or anyone else's). Heather – voted Most Likely to Be Prom Queen (also juror on the case of Breaking Up with Carl Because of Bad Haircut).

She knew every single one of them. These were her friends. She shut her locker door, jigged the padlock into place, tucked her maths folder and textbook under her arm. April came over and put her arm around Holly's shoulders. 'How about the séance, that was so cool, I'm still freaked out about your typewriter.' She steered Holly towards her first class of the day.

Holly wondered what it going to be like, sitting on the other side of the classroom from what she was used to. Being a student instead of a teacher. How was her day going to pan out? And more importantly, what sort of student was she?

8.17 am

Maths. Or, more accurately, more Americanly, math.

Mr O'Farrell walked the aisles of the classroom, collecting homework. Holly flipped frantically through her folder. There was nothing in there. No homework. Not even a page that looked like an attempt at homework. O'Farrell got to her desk and looked down at her, hand out.

'I...' Holly scrambled around inside her head. 'I left it at home.'

'Sorry, Legs,' he said, 'but you used that one last week. If you're not going to try with your homework, the least you can do is try with your excuses.'

Holly looked up at him, shocked. *Legs?* It was so openly sexist; she couldn't believe he'd just called her that. Sexist *and* inappropriate, and she was sure it violated at least [insert number] teacher/student codes. She'd never been the type to call someone out on bad behaviour but with the whole #metoo movement, she felt an obligation to say something. She couldn't let a thing like this slide.

'I'm sorry,' she said, 'what did you just call me?'

'Legs.' He didn't even have the good grace to look ashamed of himself.

'You can't call me that.'

'Okay.' He went on good-humouredly: 'I'm terribly sorry. Please accept my apology, Miss Byrne.' He bowed from the waist. 'And now, let's get back to the matter at hand. Your homework. You left it at home, you were saying?'

'Yes, that's right,' she said, not willing to relinquish her indignance just yet. 'I did the whole thing, all of it, and it's on my desk at home. I just forgot to bring it. That's all.'

She suspected that wasn't the case – she hadn't seen anything even vaguely resembling maths home-work when she'd been sifting through Trinity's papers – but when you were taking the high moral ground, it didn't do to give an inch, much less concede that you hadn't even attempted your homework.

'Excellent. In that case, I expect you'll hand it in to me first thing tomorrow morning.' O'Farrell looked down at her with a smile. 'Or Wednesday morning at the latest.'

'Absolutely,' Holly said. 'It'll be there on your desk, first thing tomorrow morning, because it's at home. Like I said. All done, all completed,' and she could hear a vague sing-song tone in her voice that she recognised from the girls she taught, the ones who didn't do their work, who put zero effort in, who didn't care.

Turned out, she was one of those.

10.43 am

English class.

Holly was sitting at a desk right up the front, centre aisle, pointed out to her by the teacher, Mrs Grimwade, when she'd walked into class. Teaching 101: put disruptive students where you could keep an eye on them.

Mrs Grimwade had her back to the class, writing on the blackboard (blackboard!), the fresh chalk letters (chalk!) stark against the green-black background.

Holly felt a tap on her shoulder, and a girl (name: Mandy; status: not a friend, just a girl in the classroom) passed over a note, indicating with a backwards tilt of the head that it had come from someone behind her.

Holly took it, unfolded the note – *Sooz says you nearly got kidnaped on Friday. True?* – then glanced back around the room to see who'd posted it.

'The answer isn't behind you,' she heard someone say at her elbow. Holly shifted around to face forward again, and found Mrs Grimwade standing in front of her desk. 'The answer should be here' – and the teacher tapped at her own temple – 'inside your brain. So please, if you'd be so kind. We were discussing Asher Lev. Illuminate us.'

Holly stared blankly. She couldn't illuminate anyone, because she didn't know what the question was and had no recollection of having read the book.

The Grim Reaper. That was what they called this woman, all bony elbows and no sense of humour.

'It's reasonable for me to assume,' the Grim Reaper continued, 'that when you're looking around the classroom, it's because you already have the answer. So tell me: why are Asher Lev's paintings considered to be less respectable than other religious paintings?' And she spread her hands wide, as if to catch Holly's wisdom in her palms.

Silence. Holly could feel the classroom watching her back. 'I don't know,' she finally mumbled.

'Excuse me?' Mrs Grimwade said, tipping her ear towards Holly and cupping it theatrically with her hand.

'I don't know,' Holly repeated. She'd dealt with enough disengaged students to know that humiliating them in front of an entire room of their peers was guaranteed to put them offside. Forever. Cupping your hand sarcastically to your ear definitely fell into that category.

'Maybe it would help if you paid more attention to what I'm writing on the blackboard, rather than what your friends are writing.' The Grim Reaper held out her hand. 'The note, please.'

'I'm sorry?'

'Hand me the note, please, Miss Byrne.'

And yes, this 'Miss Byrne' was especially sarcastic. Holly thought back to maths class. At least Mr O'Farrell's 'Miss Byrne' had held a note of humour and warmth in it. But Mrs Grimwade's held none. This woman didn't want engagement. She wanted to break Trinity.

'The note, please,' the Grim Reaper repeated, clicking her fingers impatiently.

Which was when the gut instinct of Trinity kicked in, and a steely defiance settled into her bones. 'There's no note,' Holly said, her arms folding in front of her body.

The Grim Reaper stood there, palm still out, waiting.

Holly shrugged, all innocent face and insolent shoulders. 'There's no note,' she repeated.

Mrs Grimwade simply pointed over at the door.

Holly stood up, gathered her books to her chest, and, as she walked out of the classroom, lobbed an unexpected grenade over her shoulder at Mrs Grimwade. 'I'll probably learn more out there than I would in here with you anyway.'

Holly's eyes widened a fraction, shocked at the words that had come out of her mouth. She couldn't take credit, of course; that had been pure Trinity right there. The teacher in her knew there'd be no wins on the board for being insolent, but the human being in her, the one who never called out bad behaviour, had to admire Trinity for standing up to the bully.

'And that'll be a Friday detention right there for you, young lady,' the Grim Reaper said with what could only be described as immense satisfaction.

12.27 pm

Holly sat on the bleachers overlooking the oval, fuming about Mrs Grimwade. 'Apart from anything else, it's really poor teaching method,' she said.

Susie Sioux laughed, her eyes following a group of guys running laps around the oval, her cigarette hidden under the bench. 'Poor teaching method? Seriously?' Then she scanned for teachers, took a quick drag, blew the smoke out, and hid her hand back under the bench.

Okay, maybe Holly could have rephrased it slightly, but she stood by her assessment. It was terrible teaching method, and clearly this woman had been getting away with it for years.

'I'm going to speak to the principal,' she decided. 'We shouldn't have to put up with this type of thing.'

'Oh yeah, for sure,' Aprilmayjune said, drawing in her notebook next to Heather, who had her eyes closed, face up towards the sun. 'You should *definitely* speak to the principal. They'll *definitely* listen to you. She'll be outta here so fast, her head'll spin.'

And she and Susie Sioux and Heather laughed at the very idea.

'She's been tormenting kids for years,' Heather added lazily. 'That's her MO. Why would they get rid of her? That's probably what they pay her the big bucks for. Chief Tormentor and Child Abuser.'

Holly couldn't believe these children of the seventies would accept this type of thing. Wasn't this the era of Vietnam War protests? Didn't this generation stick up for themselves?

'Okay sure, but also' – and here she was certain they'd be on her side – 'Mr O'Farrell calling me Legs is completely inappropriate.'

If either of these teachers were at Holly's school, they'd have been hauled before the Education Board by now.

'You know what,' said Heather, 'you're right. To be honest, I'm always slightly offended when he calls me Farrah.' She whipped her hair around, clearly not at all offended to be compared to Farrah Fawcett.

'Now that you mention it,' said Susie Sioux, 'I'm really upset that he calls me Boss.'

Again, not even slightly upset. Not even mildly bemused. Holly couldn't help but laugh, though. You only had to look at Susie Sioux to know why O'Farrell would call her Boss.

A ball came flying in their direction. Holly felt her reflexes reacting before she had a chance to think about it, stretching up and catching it firmly in her hand.

Susie Sioux laughed. 'Nice catch – you still got it.'

Holly looked down at the baseball in her hand. She'd never been a ball sports kind of girl, but obviously Trinity had some pretty solid skills in that area.

The pleasure of the long reach into the air, the ball finding her glove, the other fielders whooping and cheering, the hitter taking the long cold walk out of the diamond.

She shrugged as if to say *no biggie* and then threw it back to the guy down on the oval, who was looking up at her, well impressed.

Lewis.

1.56 pm

Typing class.

Mrs Dodd was a short, round little-old-lady type, wearing a woollen cardigan and sack-style skirt over thick tights with sensible shoes. She was a dead spit for one of Grannie Aileen's friends, the ones who'd come over each week and played mahjong. Or was it poker? Bridge?

Memories from Trinity's life were intruding more strongly every hour, while the memories from her own life seemed to be getting more and more remote. Like Loolah had said happened in *The Neverending Story.* Every time you made a wish, you lost a memory.

Mrs Dodd walked down the aisles of students, handing out a typewritten sheet with information about the history of chocolate in Mayan culture. 'Today, girls,' she began, because yes, everyone in the class was a girl; because yes, this was 1980 and no, boys didn't take typing classes, 'we're doing a touch-typing speed and accuracy test. I don't want anyone to worry too much about it, it's just a practice test. Simply to see how we're all going along. This doesn't go towards any grades, so just try your best. That's all I ever expect from any of you.'

Holly sat at the large clunky gunmetal-grey typewriter, her hands propped, wrists held high as if she was holding a ball under both of her hands, back straight, posture perfect. A metal barrier, like a small version of a tray for breakfast in bed, obscured the keys, just in case a student was tempted to look down at the letters instead of using the little raised nodes on the 'F' and 'J' keys to find the correct finger position. Trinity's body knew this. Same as with the guitar, the memory was in the fingers, in the arms, in the very spinal cord.

Mrs Dodd's timer went off and the entire classroom started typing text, going as quickly and as accurately as they could. There was nothing scary about this typewriter – it wasn't going to start hammering words up onto the page all by itself. It was simply typing along with her, each letter following the jab of her fingers on the obscured keys. Each full stop, each comma, exactly as she intended.

After a full minute, Mrs Dodd's timer went off for a second time and they all stopped, took their paper out of the typewriter and swapped with the girl next to them.

Holly's competitive streak felt the thrill of the point-score as she noticed that she'd done better than her neighbour. And then it occurred to her that maybe it wasn't her competitive streak: maybe it was Trinity's. This had been the only class all day that Trinity had done well in; where the body had been paying attention. In fact, it was the only class all day where Trinity's behaviour had synced up with Holly's naturally obedient nature.

For the first time, she had a glimpse of the two of them together. Blondie. Parallel lives.

3.14 pm

Holly walked out the school gates with Susie Sioux and Aprilmayjune and Heather and Lewis and Scott and Kevin and Eric and the entire cohort of students from all year levels. Freshmen siphoned out together, sophomores bunched up with sophomores. Being Australian, Holly would never have known the difference between a freshman and a sophomore, a junior and a senior, and yet here she was, instinctively able to distinguish them just by looking.

The formless mass slowly thinned out further as they walked on, until there was just her, Susie Sioux, April and Heather.

It turned out they were going shopping. Like they did every Monday. Holly wasn't sure why they went on Mondays, when most teenagers would presumably have gone shopping together on the weekend, but apparently it was their regular thing.

Holly wondered whether Trinity had replied to her letter yet, but when shopping every Monday with her best friends was what she did, she couldn't very well get out of it. In any case, she liked hanging out with these girls. They had good energy. Especially Susie Sioux, with all the ways she reminded Holly of Zoe. She missed Zoe so much, and if this was an opportunity to feel as if she was spending precious time with Zoe, she was going to take it. Trinity's letter would be sitting in the typewriter, ready to read when she got home.

But Holly found herself only half-listening to her friends' chatter. She was too distracted. What was going on back in 2020? Had Trinity received Holly's letter in the first place? Had she carried out her threat and destroyed Brother Orange? Had all communication between them ceased? Maybe Holly should have gone home, there was still—

A hand reached out and pulled Holly back, stopping her from walking out onto the road and getting bowled over by a car coming up from the left. 'Whoa. You trying to get yourself killed?' Susie Sioux said.

Holly felt her heart thrumming at the close call she'd just had. She needed to concentrate, needed to remember that cars came from the left here, not the right.

A bus pulled over and all four of them got on. Holly spent the ride looking out the window like the tourist she was – it was her first time in LA, after all – and after a few blocks, the bus pulled over and the four of them got off and walked into an enormous building, the daylight outside replaced by windowless walls and escalators and a storeys-high ceiling.

Shopping at the mall. Couldn't get more American than that.

A throw-down tantrum was being unleashed in front of a KB Toys while the mom tried to shush the kid. An old businessman was sitting on a bench watching young girls walk past. There was a 'Win a New Car!' competition, with the New Car! parked at the bottom of the escalators. There was a Sears, and an Aladdin's Castle game parlour that was all dings and flashing lights; a Camelot music shop, and a Kinney Shoes shop. There were moms holding kids' hands, and old ladies holding old husbands' hands, and arms bent at the elbows carrying shopping bags. And bad hairdos? There were a ton of them.

...old lady with bad hair and terrible clothes...

Excuse me, Holly felt like saying to Trinity, *but this, here, is bad hair and terrible clothes. Not my haircut circa 2020, very modern, very low-key, very stylish.*

They walked into a JCPenneys and the four of them fanned out, idly running their hands across the racked clothes. Holly noticed Susie Sioux slip a chunky black belt with silver studs into her schoolbag. Which was when Holly realised that this wasn't strictly a shopping expedition: it was a shoplifting expedition.

At the beginning of Grade 4, Holly, Evie and Zoe had been loitering in the comics section of a newsagent, building up to the moment when they would each put a comic in their schoolbags. But Holly worried that a whole comic would be too obvious, the difficulty rating too high for a novice. She slowly walked towards the exit, her heart thudding in her ears. But she felt like such a goody-goody that as she walked past a box of party poppers, she grabbed one and shoved it in her pocket.

The owner of the newsagent followed her outside the shop and said, 'I'd like you to turn out your pockets for me.'

Even now, in a whole other body, Holly could feel the anxiety of that day rise from her stomach to her chest. She ran her hand over her forehead. It felt clammy, hot. She needed to get out of here. She didn't want to shoplift. It wasn't her.

'What do you think of this?' Susie Sioux came over, holding up a short red dress.

'What are you gonna do?' Holly hissed at her. 'You're just going to put that in your bag?'

Susie Sioux frowned at her. 'What are you talking about?' she said, all innocent. She took in Holly's pale face. 'Are you okay?'

'I think I'm going to faint. I don't feel good.'

'Sit down here, put your head down. Wiggle your toes.'

Holly plonked down in the aisle, her arms folded across her knees, her head resting on her arms, her eyes closed. She heard Aprilmayjune and Heather come over and ask if she was okay, and when she reassured them that she was fine, they went back to rifling through the racks and holding skirts and T-shirts against their bodies. 'What do you think?' 'I'm gonna try this on.' 'This is cute.' All of them, apparently, with no intention of paying for any of it.

The shop assistant came over. 'Are you okay?' she asked.

'She feels sick,' Susie Sioux said.

Holly looked up into the young assistant's face. She was probably only twenty or something. She seemed genuinely concerned. Kind.

'I'm going to go and sit outside,' Holly said, to Susie Sioux, to the girl, to herself. She didn't want any part of it.

She sat on a bench next to the escalators, next to the Win a New Car! The mall wasn't terribly busy. And suddenly Holly had a flash of why they went shopping on Mondays instead of the weekend. Fewer customers meant fewer staff. Fewer staff meant four girls shoplifting was like shooting fish in a barrel.

After a short time, Susie Sioux came out with a shopping bag in her hand, April and Heather following. 'You feeling better?' Susie Sioux asked, putting her arm around Holly's shoulders.

Holly kept her eyes focused on her fingers, feeling slightly annoyed with these girls.

April collected Holly's chin in her hand, bringing her face around to look her straight in the eyes. She moved Holly's chin this way and that, as if examining her for flaws, checking her vital signs. 'You look better,' she finally said.

Susie Sioux held up her JCPenney shopping bag and pulled out a white T-shirt with black shells printed over it, showing it to Holly.

'You bought that?' Holly asked.

'Yeah. It's cute, don't you think?'

Holly felt all that anxiety, all that angst, evaporate from her body. All her suspicions, wrong. She'd been on edge, worried about whether Trinity had written back, and her brain was scrambling everything it saw.

They were waiting at the bus stop when April pulled up her skirt to reveal a second skirt underneath. 'By the way, I got this,' she said, looking thrilled with herself.

'And I got these,' Heather said, looking down at a brand-new pair of sandals she'd simply strapped on and walked out wearing. 'Sooz, show her what you got.'

'A little something for my collection,' said Susie Sioux, opening her schoolbag to reveal the chunky black belt that Holly had seen her pocketing earlier.

5.21 pm

Holly looked down at the typewriter on her desk and placed her fingers on the keys.

All day, her brain had been consumed with trying to keep up with the faces that swarmed in front of her, the conversations between friends, the politics of the classroom, the shoplifting at the mall. But now that she was back home, getting a letter from Trinity rose back up to number-one priority. Nothing had come through.

'Come on, Trinity,' she said, banging on the top of the typewriter as if to wake it up. 'Brother Orange – either of you! Write to me. I just want to know what's going on.'

Yesterday, when the letter from Trinity had come through and she'd replied, it had felt like they were typing to each other in real time. But now that she thought about it, there was nothing to suggest that the letters were coming through as they were being written. Trinity could have typed that letter whenever. It could have been inside Brother Orange, waiting, since before the séance, even.

Which would make sense, now that Holly thought about it. The séance had prompted the start of Trinity's letter to appear – Fuck off! – as if it could no longer contain her fury. As if it was trying to flag Holly's attention. But then it had stopped – maybe because there wasn't any paper in there? Maybe because it needed Holly sitting on her chair in front of it? Who knew? Holly was a novice when it came to this whole communicate-with-other-person-through-a-self-writing-typewriter business.

If Trinity didn't know a reply was coming through, she wouldn't necessarily have gone back to Brother Orange to check in. Maybe you needed to be near the typewriter to get a letter through? Maybe you needed to hold a séance to trigger a letter? Maybe Trinity had smashed the typewriter to pieces, just like she'd threatened. Maybe she'd never receive Holly's letter. Maybe Holly would be stuck in this life forever. Maybe, maybe, maybe, maybe maybemaybemaybemaybemaybemaybe.

She needed to distract herself. She couldn't force a letter out of the typewriter. Thinking about it over and over was sending her into a downward spiral.

She went over to lie on the bed, her back to the desk. She thought about the maths homework she was supposed to have done. That shouldn't be too hard. She'd always been good at maths. Maths and art, opposing subjects, her two favourites. She would cook up a little something to hand in to O'Farrell tomorrow, along with the advice that he shouldn't call her Legs anymore. She sat back up, cross-legged, and dragged her Pan Am bag over. Took the maths folder and textbook out, balanced the folder on her knees and started reading.

'Draw pie charts to represent the following data,' she read aloud. She loved pie charts. They were so… visual. 'Twenty-four people divided into five different jobs: eight doctors, two nurses, six lawyers, two police officers, six teachers. Write the percentage of people who hold each job.' That should be easy enough. Although, how did you work it out? She hadn't done maths in years, not since Year 12, and as it turned out, she hadn't retained as much of it as she would have thought. Nothing was coming to her. There must be a formula she was supposed to be using. She flipped through the maths textbook but struggled to find anything of use.

She pushed the maths books away and decided to tackle English instead. *My Name Is Asher Lev* was plonked on top of a pile of other books in the bookcase, the spine suspiciously pristine. It seemed Trinity hadn't even bothered reading the book. Holly started reading. Two paragraphs in, she set the book down.

She couldn't settle. The words were floating, the sentences didn't hold together.

She reached over and picked up the acoustic guitar that was propped beside the wardrobe, her focus on those six strings taking all other thoughts away, the sounds she produced calming her entire body down. But then something made her glance at the typewriter. Not a noise so much as a movement. A fluttering that caught her attention. If she had to describe it, she'd say the keys seemed to be simmering, like a pot on the stove.

She put the guitar back down and moved over to the desk, gingerly touched the keys – they felt warm. She typed a single random letter just to get it started:

O—

And the typewriter took off, same as yesterday, clattering at a million miles an hour, savagery tearing out of the orange enamelled body.

Oh yeah, yeah, you're going to FIX MY LIFE?!? Forget it!!! Your life's gonna be well and truly trashed if you don't fix things NOW! I've seen your house I've seen all your space age stuff obviously you're a scientist and you made this happen. I don't care how you did it, or why you did it, or how you used my typewriter to do it, but I'm telling you right now, you better fix things back the way they were, old lady. NOW.

The good news was that it appeared Trinity had finally received Holly's letter.

And don't you dare touch my life. Don't touch a single hair on my life. It's perfect the way it is. In fact, maybe I'm here to fix your life you ever thought of that? And I'm gonna fix it, real good, unless you SWAP US BACK! Some news: your work rang on some weird little phone that I found in your tote just now, and they asked where I was today, and now that I think about it, going to your work and doing your job is just one of the ways I can FIX YOUR LIFE. So I'm warning you, you better swap us back right now. Right NOW. And you can fuck right off with doing seances with my friends. You're not to go anywhere near them. Not Susie Sioux or April or Lewis or my family or anything in my life, I swear.

Suddenly the typewriter slid away from Holly and banged against the wall under the window as if it had been shoved. As if, by the sheer force of her outrage, Trinity's push from the future had acted on Brother Orange here in Holly's present.

And then, a cavernous silence.

Holly brought the typewriter back towards her and re-read the letter, trying to settle the shaking that was vibrating through her body, boiling her blood. The anger Trinity was directing at her felt like it was coming not only from Brother Orange, but from inside this very body itself.

Holly stood up and began to pace in front of the desk. She had to work out how to respond. She needed to calm Trinity down. She needed to think.

Her feet carried her downstairs and out the front door. She started walking the block, a walk that soon turned into a run. The rhythm of her feet hitting the pavement, heel toe, heel toe, was such a simple thing to focus on. Each step propelled her body, and the coldness of the air in her throat burned as she inhaled. She'd never been much of a runner, always more of a swimmer before swapping over to karate in her thirties, but for this girl, this body, running was her jam. The loping gait felt effortless. There was the sense that she could run for hours. And the energy inside this body. Holly had forgotten how it was to be sixteen, to feel alive, awake, switched on, day after day after day.

Holly felt a desire to be let off the leash. Not to let Trinity off the leash, but herself. All these years, she'd tried to do what she thought others had wanted from her. But why? What for? It hadn't made any difference to anyone. All her life she'd constrained her soul, tied it up tight, choosing the safe options every time. A teaching degree instead of fine art, Melbourne instead of Paris. But now, as she experienced the joy of this body in flight, she realised that she'd always done wrong by herself. This girl knew how to live. How to feel. Even the letter Trinity had typed in reply to Holly's, even the abuse she'd hurled, showed that at least she was feeling stuff. Living life. Being herself.

By the time Holly got back to her street (Trinity's street), she was sweating and hot, panting, tired, but she knew exactly what she wanted to type in reply.

When she walked in the back door, the mom was at the stove, putting spaghetti into a big pot.

'You've been for a run,' the mom said. 'How was it?'

'It was good.'

'It's been a while – how's your fitness?'

Holly laughed. 'Fine.'

'Dinner's nearly ready.'

'I'll set the table,' Holly said and registered the mom's eyebrows shoot up at the offer. 'I've just gotta type something up and then I'll be straight back down. Is that okay?'

'Sure. I'd really appreciate that.'

Holly ran back up the stairs, rolled in a fresh piece of paper and started typing.

Trinity. Please, just hang on a sec. Everything's exactly the same in your life as when you left it. I haven't done anything. You have a lovely life, and I didn't mean I was going to change anything. I was just trying to figure out a reason for the swap to have happened. Anyway, never mind. I'm not here to fix your life. Forget I ever said it.

Maybe she should mention the guy who'd picked Trinity up that first afternoon and tried to put her in his car. Check if he might be the reason for the soul swap? Although anything that sounded like she was going to 'fix' things was likely to set Trinity off. No, this wasn't the time for information-sharing – this was damage control, pure and simple.

You seem to think I organised this swap somehow, but I promise, I didn't. I'm just as confused as you are. I'm not a scientist. I'm an ordinary art teacher. Nothing like this has ever happened in my life.

We're in this together. You and me, kiddo, she nearly typed, but decided it might come off as patronising.

I also think it's really important that you don't destroy the typewriter. I know you're angry, but if Brother Orange can't type, there's every chance we won't be able to communicate with each other anymore, and then maybe we will stay this way forever, and I'm pretty sure you don't want that.

Good point. Important to make that clear. *You want things to go back to the way they were? Pull your head in.*

You said my work rang? Maybe you should call in sick tomorrow. The phone number is in my mobile under S for St Luke's. (I'm guessing you've figured out how to use my phone in the same way I seem to know how to use things in your life, kind of instinctively.) Maybe it's best that you don't leave the house.

How about you stay inside...

Preferably with the blinds closed.

...and I'll try to sort things out for both of us. There's plenty of food in the fridge. And the freezer. I always make my meals a week in advance, so you won't starve!

Always good to end with some friendly humour.

I'll write again tomorrow and see how you're feeling.

Don't leave the house, whatever you do.

Bye!

Cheery! Bright! I'm your friend! We're in this together! Calm the fuck down!

Holly

6.12 pm

Holly twisted the spaghetti around her fork. The empty tin of bolognaise sauce was still on the bench. She couldn't believe how badly this family ate, especially seeing as the mom worked in health. But actually, it tasted a lot better than you'd expect. Salty and flavoursome and no doubt full of dodgy fats.

'So how's this for a coincidence,' the mom said. 'I forgot to tell you. On Friday, I was assisting in the delivery of a little leap-year baby, same as you...'

Holly stared at the mom. She'd been so busy fumbling her way through all the trips and hazards of living a stranger's life and figuring out how to fix everything that she hadn't given any thought to the baby-her who would have been born last week. Until this moment.

'...and this morning I was checking her chart,' the mom continued, 'and I noticed that she's Rhnull. Same blood type as you. Same birthday, same blood type. Even born ten weeks prem. What are the chances?'

Holly could barely swallow past the lump in her throat. Most people hadn't heard of Rhnull, or 'golden blood', because it was so rare. But anyone who had it knew all about it. Only 0.0000006 per cent of the population were Rhnull. Forty-three people in the whole world.

Holly had grown up knowing she had golden blood. That she'd been born ten weeks premature. A leap-year baby. In Los Angeles.

What were the chances indeed?

'Obviously we should have some in reserve for bub,' the mom was going on. 'So if you come to the hospital tomorrow, we'll get a blood donation organised. Dad can drop you off after your driving lesson.'

This was impossible. It was definitely too much of a coincidence. But Holly couldn't not ask. 'What's the baby's name?'

The mom looked at her and laughed. 'Trinity. Her name's Trinity, same as you. I mean, talk about coincidence!'

Holly felt her shoulders release the tension. It wasn't her. It was someone else's leap-year baby. And then the mom laughed again.

'No, I'm kidding. That would be too much of a coincidence. Her name's Holly.'

Holly's chest felt constricted and painful, like a fist was gripping her heart and squeezing tight.

'Like my doll,' Loolah said.

The mom nodded. 'Yes. Exactly.'

'Maybe I should give it to her?' Loolah wondered. 'I'm getting a bit too old for dolls.'

The Holly Hobbie under the stairs at her house. Had Loolah given it to her?

'I feel sorry for the mom,' Trinity's mom was saying. 'She's only young, and it's never easy having your baby in intensive care. And the whole rare-blood thing makes it ten times more stressful. But on top of everything, she's really struggling because she's on her own.'

'Because she's from Australia,' Holly said, mainly to herself. Everything was clicking into place like balls in a slot machine.

The mom looked across at her. 'Yes...' she said.

'Whoa,' Loolah said.

Holly looked from one to the other, knowing an explanation was needed. 'Well, that's what you said earlier, wasn't it?'

'No,' the mom said.

'No,' Loolah said.

'Yes. You definitely said she was from Australia. Otherwise, how would I know?'

And the mom and Loolah had no good comeback.

Frances and Nathan had met in Morocco and fallen in love, like in all good backpacking romances. They'd exchanged addresses, then continued travelling separately. It wasn't until months later that Frances realised maybe she hadn't had a period in a while. That she was putting on weight. She'd done an over-the-counter pregnancy test (positive) and had gone to a Dutch doctor only to discover she was nearly six months gone. Panicking slightly, she'd booked herself a flight home to Australia, but decided she had time to stop off via America first. By the time she'd arrived in Los Angeles, she was nearly seven months along. She'd turned up at the address Nathan had given her, where she learnt that he'd fallen off a balcony in Whistler a month earlier and died. Frances had gone into labour right there on the doorstep and had to be rushed to hospital. Her baby was born on 29 February 1980 in Los Angeles, ten weeks premature, a little girl called Holly with Rhnull blood.

Little baby-her had been delivered by Trinity's mom and was in a hospital somewhere in this sprawling city. And tomorrow Holly was going to donate blood to her very own baby-self.

That was the connection. The final piece of the puzzle. The life she'd been sent to fix – it wasn't Trinity's. It was baby-hers.

She'd been sent her to change her whole entire future.

Day 5

TUESDAY,
4 MARCH
1980

7.23 am

Lewis sat at the breakfast bench, shovelling cereal into his mouth. 'That was a killer catch yesterday,' he said.

Holly nodded. 'Yeah, no, you're right. It seriously was.' She didn't even feel like she was bragging, because after all, it wasn't even her body. And it *was* a killer catch. She was only calling it as she saw it.

'It's not too late for you to start training again, you know,' he said. 'They only started back a couple of weeks ago.'

She wondered why Trinity had given up softball. And running. It didn't make sense. The feeling of that ball smacking into her hand, the thrill of the catch, the joy of running on the pavement. These were all things this girl got a buzz out of. But for some reason she wasn't doing them anymore.

'How'd you go with the rest of your homework, by the way?' Lewis went on. 'Dog didn't eat it?'

'Don't have a dog. Do I?' Holly wondered if maybe there was a dog hidden somewhere that she hadn't noticed yet.

'That hasn't stopped you before.'

Holly registered the sarcasm but chose to ignore it. 'I pretty much answered none of the maths questions—'

'"Maths"?' Lewis said, raising an eyebrow.

'*Math* questions,' she said. American American. 'And I haven't even finished reading *Asher Lev* yet, so, yeah…'

'You should have come over last night. I would have helped you. Alternatively, we could have tried to find you a dog.'

Holly laughed.

She like the way his mouth turned up at the edges, like he was constantly on the verge of laughing out loud. The mischievousness that sparkled in his eyes. The way she sometimes caught him looking at her. She had to remind herself that she was old enough to be his mother, and that even to be thinking such thoughts was completely grotesque. Besides, they were just friends. She was sure of it.

She'd seen him come out of the house next door, skateboard in hand. Watched him set off as if he had a million places to be and a million people to see. Susie Sioux and April came over, and the three of them were sitting on the front lawn in the sunshine when he got back home. Of course they introduced themselves. 'My stepdad got a job at Universal, so the whole family's moved over,' he told them in his cute Australian accent. Afterwards, the girls had joked that it was like Grease *in reverse – the role of Sandy to be played by a blond, handsome blue-eyed Aussie guy instead of Olivia Newton-John. And don't worry, there were plenty of girls itching to play the part of John Travolta. But Trinity had refused to have a crush on him because that would have been clichéd, and she was all about busting stereotypes, not slavishly following them. Although, okay sure, if he'd insisted . . . Except then he'd started going out with that girl Bridget from the Catholic school, and by the time he'd broken up with her a few months later the two of them, him and Trinity, had gone too far down the friendship route.*

The mom came into the kitchen. 'Hi, Lewis,' she said.

'Hi, Mrs B.'

'Don't forget,' she said, turning to Holly, 'Dad'll be picking you up from school and taking you for a driving lesson. Then get him to bring you to the hospital. We'll grab some of your blood for that baby, and you can go back to his place for dinner after.' Then she walked back out.

Holly flipped from thinking about Lewis to thinking about the hugeness of changing the entire future of her baby-self. Her nerves rose like bees disturbed from their flowers.

Her reason for being here. To fix her own life.

Plus a driving lesson with the dad. Just the two of them in the car together.

Every day there was some new chunk of enormousness to think about.

Lewis intruded on her thoughts. 'You put on such a tough act,' he said, 'and then you go and do something like that. Donate blood.' And he pushed a strand of hair behind her ear.

The surprisingly intimate move had Holly's breath catching in her chest. She gave herself a mental shake. He was younger than her. *Much* younger. Besides, he didn't even know her. She was a pretender. She wasn't this person. 'I've gotta go brush my teeth,' she said and ran up the stairs, away from him.

Or maybe she was running away from herself. She couldn't quite decide.

9.42 am

Holly sat herself down in the front row – her Grim-Reaper-designated spot – and wondered how things would go at the hospital that afternoon. Technically, she was giving blood, no big deal, she'd done it plenty of times before. When you had Rhnull blood, you donated regularly, trying to keep some in reserve for yourself in case you ever needed it. But obviously this time was way bigger of a deal, way more significant.

And suddenly a new thought fell into her brain. Frances would be at the hospital. Her mum. They might run into each other and get chatting, and Holly might say the magic words that would make Frances a better mum. It felt like a crazy thing to even contemplate, but if a butterfly in the Amazon could create a hurricane in Texas, then going back in time and turning up at the hospital where your baby-self had just been born *had* to have consequences.

She needed to be prepared. Needed to have the exact right thing to say ready in her back pocket in case she ran into Frances. But what would she say? Holly sat with her chin in her palm and ran through a couple of scenarios.

You can be a great mum to your little girl, but you need to be there with her, not leave her with her grannie. She doubted that would make a flea's bit of a difference.

Every baby needs their mum. You can make or break that little girl. Again, no.

Something better. Something more inspiring and perfect. Something future-changing. Something…

'Homework?' she heard someone say at her elbow. Holly glanced up, then flopped her hand back down onto her desk.

It was the Grim Reaper.

She didn't have any homework to hand in because she'd only got a couple of pages into *Asher Lev*. It had been impossible to concentrate on anything after hearing that she would be donating blood to her baby-self. She had nothing, and the Grim Reaper was standing there, looking down at her.

'I'm sorry, Mrs Grimwade,' Holly said, sucking in Trinity's natural inclination for sarcasm. The best way to deal with a teacher like this was with politeness and honesty. That was what she'd done, all those years back when she was at school. Although, of course, she'd always read the books and done the homework, so maybe her experience didn't quite relate. 'I haven't read the book yet. And I haven't done my homework.'

'Well,' the Reaper said, arms folded. 'I guess I should be pleased that you're at least being honest for once.'

See, it did work. Although the 'for once' was typically and unnecessarily snarky.

'So what do you propose we do?' the Reaper asked.

Holly looked up at her. There was an obvious answer. 'Well, I guess I need an extension.'

Mrs Grimwade's mouth pulled back into a tight approximation of a smile. 'So everyone else in the class has managed to complete their homework and handed it in on time, but for you, I should make an exception and grant an extension?'

'If that's okay with you.'

'And what if it's not okay with me?' the Reaper said, eyebrows raised.

Holly looked up at this woman who was determined to play hardball, who wouldn't give an inch. Who, when faced with plain, bare-faced honesty, still had to go for the nasty response.

Holly had bigger fish to fry. She was going to be seeing Frances this afternoon. She was going to be donating blood to her very own baby-self. She didn't have the brain space to think about this. Mrs Grimwade had no clue about the things she was up against. 'I don't know,' Holly said. 'What happens if it's not okay with you?' And the way *not okay* came out of her mouth, all sarcastic and stretched out, meant another Friday detention was inevitable.

12.22 pm

Holly couldn't concentrate on what Susie Sioux was saying, something about band rehearsal for her party. April mentioned she'd bring her drum kit around. Her friends were talking, there was the *thwock* and yell of lunchtime sport on the oval, but everything everyone was saying sounded muffled and distant. Her mind was spinning.

What would she say to Frances? How could she fix things here, in 1980, so that her own future would be happier? What sorts of things did she want to change? Obviously having Frances more involved would be a start. But she didn't want Grannie Aileen to be less involved. Maybe the three of them could live together, with Frances not out all the time, *as per usual.*

Holly put a hand on her knee to still the bouncing. She needed to move. Sitting around doing nothing wasn't helping. A run had helped yesterday. 'I'll be back,' she mumbled, and without waiting for a response, she got up from the bench and stepped down the bleachers towards the oval. As she walked the perimeter, she noticed some girls throwing a ball around. The softball team. Holly walked closer, unsure if she'd recognise the coach, but when she saw her, she knew exactly who it was.

'Hey, coach,' she said, coming to a stop next to her.

The coach barely gave her a glance, instead keeping her gaze on the team. Classic Teacher Freezer pose. She was obviously annoyed with Trinity for ditching softball.

Together, they watched the girls going through their paces, pitching balls, practising swings, running and sliding to base.

It had been a good shot. She ran through first base, hesitating for a fraction of a moment before bolting for second. When she realised she risked being caught out, she turned back to first but caught her foot awkwardly and flipped down onto her shoulder. Pain burst along her collarbone. She lay there quietly, not moving, assessing whether she'd done any damage. She was quickly surrounded by her teammates, and Coach came on-field to check on her. As she went to stand up she fell slightly forward and put her arm out instinctively to catch herself. That was when they all heard the crack, *and searing pain ripped through Trinity's shoulder. She looked down to see the broken bone poking up hard against the fabric of her skin.*

Holly touched her fingers up to the collarbone, the bump where Trinity's bone had knitted together, the memory running parallel with another memory, a dual screen.

She'd been playing footy and the girl from the Mount Waverley team had slung her to the ground in an illegal tackle. Suddenly, it was all searing pain and a broken bone poking at her skin. She was quickly surrounded by her teammates; Grannie Aileen ran out onto the ground. The operation kept her off the footy field for six weeks, and by the time she was due to go back she'd lost her nerve.

She and Trinity had both broken their collarbone. Holly understood the reluctance Trinity felt at going back to it. The pain of the break, the feel of the bone against skin. Both memories caused a visceral body reaction in her. But Holly had always lived a scared kind of life, and she wasn't going to let Trinity make the same mistake.

Finally, after a few minutes watching the girls practise, the coach turned towards Holly. 'You still here?' she asked, teasing, an eyebrow raised.

It wouldn't have hurt her to ask how the collarbone was. 'I was thinking I wouldn't mind joining the team again,' Holly said.

Coach didn't say anything for a moment, just looked back over at the girls, her face straight. Holly knew it: Coach's old no-expression face. A dead giveaway that she was thrilled to have Trinity back on the team. 'All right,' Coach finally said. 'We'll see you Thursday for practice.'

And just like that, Holly ticked the 'Sport: Fixed' box.
You're very welcome, Trinity. You can thank me later.

3.07 pm

Holly stood out the front of John Marshall High School, looking for the dad driving a car of some description. He wasn't there, but then she remembered he always picked her up in Aloha Street. Around the corner in Aloha, a blue car with a white vinyl roof and GT stripe down the side was waiting for her. The dad was leaning against the passenger-side door, his arms folded across his chest, watching her as she walked towards him. He looked at her as if she was a little bit sparkly. Like he absolutely adored her. He gave her a casual kiss, as though this was perfectly normal, like he was her dad and she was his daughter.

No, Holly felt like saying to him, *this is major, this is amazing, this is not normal, you don't understand how lucky this girl is.*

'You ready?' he asked her.

Holly nodded.

She could hear Trinity's regular response, *Ready for nothin'*, playing inside her head, but she couldn't quite manage it. It wasn't hers to say.

The dad looked at her a moment, noticing the omission, then decided against saying anything. Instead he opened the passenger-side door (which was on the wrong side of the car, by the way) and hopped in. Holly remained standing next to the unfamiliar car, nervous.

'Come on, slow coach,' the dad called out, looking across at her through the driver's-side window. 'We haven't got all day.' And he honked the horn to make his point.

Holly opened the door and settled herself into the driver's seat (on the wrong side). Checked the rear-view mirror, cranked down the window. Turned the key in the ignition. The dad had his arm resting out the window, tapping against the doorframe in time to some unidentifiable song on the radio. She looked down and froze. A gearstick. The car was a manual. Her car, back in 2020, was an automatic. She'd never driven a manual in her life. But now, here she was, behind the wheel of a stick shift with no clue what to do next. How many lessons had Trinity had? How well did she know how to drive? Holly just had to trust that this body knew what it was doing.

'Today,' the dad said. 'Be nice to get going sometime today.'

Holly took a deep breath and tried to centre herself. She pushed the knob of the radio in, so she didn't get distracted by the music.

The dad side-glanced at her.

'I don't really remember how to put it in reverse,' she said.

The dad laughed. 'You're not exactly filling me with confidence,' he said.

'Yeah? Me neither.'

'You got the clutch in?'

Holly pushed the clutch all the way down to the floor with her left foot, and the dad put his hand over hers, pushing the gearstick down, then firmly into reverse. 'Remember?' he said.

No, she didn't. But yes, she did. There was a small degree of muscle memory built up in the body, but because she was still a learner driver, it wasn't deep in the bones yet.

They drove through the streets of Los Feliz. She went for the indicators on the wrong side, forgot to check the rear-view mirrors, took a corner too tightly, mounted the kerb, turned into oncoming traffic. All to a very measured commentary from the dad, the calmness of his voice betrayed by the fact that his foot kept pumping away at an imaginary brake pedal, and his hands kept bracing against the dashboard in self-protection mode every time they turned a corner.

The dad suggested she turn into a half-empty carpark so she could practise her parking. Reverse-parking a monstrously long car when she was used to driving a Mazda 3 felt like she was sliding in mud with skis for wheels. After attempts of varying success, the dad got out of the car and walked around to the driver's side.

'And that's a wrap. Good job.' He banged the roof of the car in over-enthusiastic emphasis. 'You probably need a bit more work on your reversing, and a few times you were driving on the wrong side of the road, and the time you mounted the kerb wasn't ideal, but otherwise it was all good. But it might be easier for me to drive you to the hospital. There'll be traffic, and it could be hard to find a park.'

Holly couldn't have agreed more.

3.56 pm

The dad pulled over to drop her off at St Anne's. 'I expect you'll be a while,' he said, 'so get Mom to give me a call at work once you've finished, and I'll swing by and pick you back up.' With a last wave and a last smile, he drove off.

Holly felt tension rising in her shoulders as she walked up through the double front doors into the foyer. She went over to the woman sitting in reception, told her she was waiting for Nurse Byrne, then sat on one of the plastic chairs, waiting for the mom to come get her. Frances was somewhere in this building. Maybe Holly would see her wandering into the cafeteria, or going to the gift shop. Or perhaps heading out for some fresh air. Each time the lift dinged, Holly looked up. Each time the front doors were pushed open, she looked over. She couldn't imagine how it would be to see Frances in this place. She cycled between not wanting to see her, being scared at the very thought of it, and feeling a desperate hunger to see her, to talk to her, to say the one perfect thing that would turn Frances into the mum Holly had always wished she'd be.

A young couple came in through the front doors – the wife slim and neatly made up, the husband in a suit. A young girl, a teenager, came out of the lifts and nearly walked straight into them. Polite apologies ensued. A heavily pregnant teen girl came in with probably her mom.

Another teenage girl came out of the lift and walked over to the public phone. Holly stared at her and felt her breath catch in her ribs. She wasn't a teenager, she was twenty years old. Her hair was long, shaggy, mousy-coloured, the fringe flicking away from her face. A collection of fine gold chains hung around her neck. Her jeans were flared and she was wearing a Carter–Mondale T-shirt. There were shadows under her eyes. She looked drained, exhausted, emotional.

Frances.

Holly felt a hand on her arm. Startled, she turned to see the mom looking at her. Trinity's mom.

'You okay?' the mom asked.

Holly's hand dropped back to her side like she'd been caught stealing something. She hadn't even noticed until that moment that it was outstretched, reaching towards Frances. Holly stared over to where Frances was now talking to someone on the pay phone.

The very few photos of her and Frances together had all been framed and placed on the bookshelf in the front room at home. There was one of them in front of the lion enclosure at Melbourne Zoo. In another, a toddler-Holly was snuggled up on Frances's lap at a table out in the sun. One last photo, this time showing Frances with her entire body covered with sand as Holly knelt beside her, grinning up at the camera, pleased with her work at burying her mum.

Sometimes she'd been there – Holly had the framed photos to prove it. She wasn't always absent. *As per usual* hadn't always been the case.

She should go over to Frances, say something to her. What if she never saw her again? This might be her only chance. This might be the opportunity the universe was putting in front of her. But what would she say? What would make Frances listen?

Your name is Frances and I'm Holly. I'm your baby, up in the nursery, the one you had on Friday. You need to be a better mum to me. I missed out on you. You weren't around enough. Yeah. No. That wouldn't cut it.

Trinity's mom threaded her arm through Holly's, and together they walked over to the lifts. Got in. The doors shut. Holly wanted to put the brakes on, insist she needed to go and speak to Frances. But how to explain to Trinity's mom?

The good news was, Holly had seen Frances. She was here. In this building. She would go find her straight after giving blood. She'd get her room number from reception. She'd sit down with her and they'd chat, and in the moment, Holly would find the exact right perfect thing to say.

Of course, Holly had always known how young Frances had been, but she hadn't really registered until this moment how *very* young she was. Twenty years old. There in the flesh, she looked like some of the seniors Trinity went to school with, some of the Year 12s Holly taught. No wonder she'd struggled. No wonder she'd preferred to go off for days at a time 'partying', as Grannie Aileen had put it. *As per usual.*

'Julie's going to do it,' the mom was saying as they got out of the lift and walked down the corridor to a room with curtained cubicles. 'She's got a gentle touch. Best with the IVs.'

It wasn't Frances's fault. Frances hadn't wanted a baby in the first place. She'd fallen pregnant by accident. And she'd kept the baby – that had to mean something. She must have started out with good intentions. But the years must had drilled them down, grinding them to dust.

'Julie, this is my daughter Trinity…'

But now Holly had a chance to change things.

Julie put a needle into her arm and hooked the plastic bag up to a pole to collect her rare blood. Golden blood. That was the sound of destiny, right there.

4.41 pm

Holly followed Trinity's mom back down the corridor towards the lifts, heading for reception. She'd just given a pint of golden blood to her baby-self. It was enough to explode her head. She wished there was someone she could talk to about it, but there was no one. Not April or Susie Sioux or Lewis or any of them. Trinity's mom? No. She couldn't. Right from day one, she'd known no one in this world would believe her. She didn't even need to run through the conversation inside her head to know how unbelievable it sounded. There was no way of framing it that wouldn't lead to some pretty serious, concerned, sceptical faces.

She wondered how baby-her was doing. Was she awake? Was she gurgling or crying, happy or anxious? Kicking her blankets off, gripping a finger, sucking her thumb, ready for a bath? Frances might be with her right this very moment. The thought of seeing the two of them together – mother and baby – made Holly's heart lurch. A fresh start without all the history that was yet to come. Here she was, at the very beginning of it all. A once-in-a-thousand-years opportunity.

'Can I go visit her?'

'Visit who?' the mom asked.

'The baby. The one's who's getting my blood.'

The mom looked as if she was going to say no, but then she shrugged. 'Sure. Why not.' She pushed the lift button to go up, not down.

Holly's breathing was shallow. She could feel the pulse of blood in her ears. She was unsure whether what she was feeling was extreme anxiety or extreme excitement. Probably both. How would it feel to look down upon herself as a baby?

They walked into an anteroom where a long sink ran along one wall, a sign above the sink instructing every visitor to wash their hands thoroughly.

She was early for her birthday lunch with Evie and had spent the wait time scrolling through news articles on her phone. Coronavirus had reached pandemic proportions in some countries. Everyone was being told to wash their hands thoroughly to stop the spread. Evie walked into the restaurant and the two of them bumped elbows as a joke, before hugging. It was hard to take it seriously in Australia. They were so far away.

As Holly stood at the long sink, working the soap into the creases of her fingers, she felt a pang of anxiety about her actual future in 2020. She'd been so preoccupied with what was going on here in 1980, with what she'd missed out on as a child growing up, but what would happen to 2020-her if she interfered in her own past? If – as she was about to do – she met herself as a baby?

She thought about all the time-travel movies she'd seen – *Back to the Future* and *The Time Traveller's Wife* and even, maybe, *17 Again*. You never wanted to come face to face with your future (or past) self. It might have dire consequences, cause some kind of rip in the space–time continuum.

She shouldn't have come. She should leave. She shouldn't risk it. But through the doorway, tantalisingly close, she could see a single row of plastic humidicribs. Four of them. Baby-her was in one of them.

The mom walked into the intensive care unit, and Holly followed behind, as if drawn by a magnet. The first humidicrib had a baby the size of a twig. The next crib held an enormous baby, barely fitting inside the plastic box. Another tiny little bird of a thing slept in the third one, and finally, in the last humidicrib in the row, was her baby-self.

She was miniscule. A tube was up her nose, pumping oxygen straight into her lungs. Another tube ran down her throat, drip-feeding her. She was lying on her back, eyes closed, looking frail, breakable. Vulnerable. She wasn't gurgling or kicking off blankets or sucking a thumb. She was too small, too premature, to be doing any of that.

Sitting in the corner at her feet was Loolah's Holly Hobbie doll.

Holly watched baby-her's chest rise and fall, rise and fall, and realised that she was breathing in synchronicity. A shiver ran down her back, and she noticed that baby-her shivered also. She felt tears welling, and baby-her started crying – not a fully-fledged baby cry, but a tiny squawk, as much as the tiny lungs could muster.

'She's the dearest little thing,' the mom was saying, completely absorbed by the fragile human in the plastic box. 'An absolute dot.'

Holly put her palm flat against the outside of the humidicrib and watched as baby-her, eyes still closed, stretched out in a yawn, the tiniest hand, with five of the smallest fingers she'd ever seen, reaching towards her.

Holly's tears fell. The mom put an arm around her and whispered, 'I know. I remember the first time I saw one of these little preemie babies.' The word 'preemie' contrasted with the Australian 'premmie' that Holly had grown up hearing. 'It seems impossible that a tot this small will survive. But they do. They're strong. Just like you were. Ten weeks early, same as you. And look at you now: you've grown up to be so strong. You're a fighter. And that's a good thing. Sometimes I wish there was less of the fighting' – a little joke – 'but I guess I've got to take the good with the bad. I wouldn't change a thing.'

Holly turned towards this lovely woman and sobbed into her shoulder, Trinity's mom shushing her gently – 'You're okay, you're okay,' over and over – until Holly absorbed the words and knew that actually, yes, she was okay.

5.08 pm

'I'll call Dad and let him know you've finished,' the mom said. 'He'll probably be here in twenty minutes, half an hour? And then I'll pick you up from his place a little before nine.' She gave Holly a hug goodbye. 'Have a nice time.'

Holly smiled and waved as the mom headed off down the corridor. As soon as the mom turned the corner, she dropped her arm and the smile. She didn't have much time.

Taking the lift to the ground floor, Holly headed over to reception. She was still grappling with the enormity of having seen her very own baby self. It had been incredible. For the first time, she had a real sense of how hard it must have been for Frances, to see that little baby lying there, raw-skinned and plugged into tubes and beeping monitors, and only being allowed to look, not touch. 'They're very vulnerable to infections,' the mom had told her. 'Until their skin is properly formed, we have to be careful. It's hard for the moms, not being able to pick up and cuddle their babies. It makes it hard for them to bond.'

'She called me from the hospital the day you were born, all the way over in LA,' Grannie Aileen had told Holly, after Frances had died. 'The doctors didn't think you'd make it. And she'd just found out the terrible news about Nathan. The ski accident. She was so distressed. Told me she hadn't even been able to do the most basic job of keeping her baby inside to full-term. I'm not making excuses for her, but I think that's why she left you with me a lot. She felt she was no good at looking after you.'

'Okay, yeah sure, maybe,' Holly said. 'But I survived. I grew up. You can't blame me being prem, for her not being around to look after me.'

Holly *had* always felt like it was her fault. But this was her chance to fix it. As soon as she got home, she'd write a letter and tell Trinity all about the golden blood and donating to her baby-self. Maybe Trinity would feel better knowing it was Holly's life, not hers, that needed to be fixed, and that once she'd sorted out whatever it was she had to sort out, they'd be swapped back. At least, that was what Holly assumed. Hoped.

The receptionist looked up at her. 'Can I help you?' she asked.

'I'd like the room number for Frances Fitzgerald, thanks,' Holly said. She wasn't even sure if the receptionist would give it to her. Would she have to prove they had a relationship? Would the nurse ask for proof of ID?

But the woman said nothing, simply checked a register – a typewritten sheet in a school folder – then looked back up at Holly. 'Sorry, doll, she's already been discharged.'

Holly took a step back, as if pushed. 'But that can't be right,' she said. 'I saw her this afternoon. Her baby's still here. Upstairs. I was just with her.'

'Let's see...yes. Baby'll be here for another few weeks yet. The mom was discharged on...' The receptionist consulted the register again. 'Yesterday.'

Holly's entire throat plugged up. She should have grabbed Frances earlier when she saw her heading to the pay phone. That had been her one opportunity to fix things. Instead, she'd gone and donated blood, walked off like the obedient doormat she'd always been. It was cruel. The universe was playing a huge joke on her.

'Are you okay?' the receptionist asked.

Holly didn't even answer; instead she turned away and walked out the hospital entrance, feeling as distressed as

Frances had looked earlier. She walked down the street, not even sure where she was heading.

Which was when she saw her. Correction. Saw them.

Frances. Her mum. With Nathan King. Her dad.

The photo of the two of them in Morocco, their faces crinkled into smiles and their hands up to shield their eyes from the sun. That – along with the box under the stairs that held the letters they'd written to each other – was all Holly had of the two of them together.

But he'd died on a ski trip in Canada before Frances had even landed in America. That was why Frances had gone into premature labour – from the shock of hearing he'd fallen off the balcony in Whistler. And yet here he was, opening the passenger-side door of a long, boaty American car for Frances.

Holly ran over and stood there dumbly, staring at the two of them. She could feel her mouth opening, then closing, but no words came out. *You lied*, she felt like screaming at Frances. *You said he died, but here he is.* All she managed to squeeze out was, 'It's you. You're here.'

The two of them looked over at Holly.

Nathan stared at her for one click, his face blank, before walking over to the driver's side of the car and opening his door. But then he stopped and did a double-take; frowned, as if she was familiar to him.

As if she was family.

The flash of something like recognition strobed across his face for a moment before he shut it back down again.

Questions flooded Holly's brain: If he was alive, why had Frances left America on her own? Why had she told everyone he'd died? If he'd come to Australia, or Frances had stayed here in America, Holly's life would have been so different. She would have had a mum and a dad.

'I'm sorry. Do I know you?' Frances said, shocking Holly with the realisation that while she knew Frances so well, Frances had no clue who she was.

Look at me. I'm your daughter. You know me. You must recognise my soul, at the very least.

'Have we met?' Frances continued. She had her hand resting on the car door, as if she was teetering on the brink of getting in the car or staying there on the kerb and listening. It just depended on what Holly said next.

'No, okay, so you don't exactly know me…it's complicated,' Holly stammered, on the back foot. What was she supposed to say next? How was she to make them both listen? She hadn't rehearsed this. She'd been picturing Frances. Not Frances and Nathan. She felt all akimbo, every thought blasted out of her head.

Frances's chin trembled slightly, like she was about to start crying. She assessed Holly, then made the decision to get into the car. 'I'm sorry,' she said, 'but today's not a good day.'

She went to shut the passenger door.

'Wait!' Holly said, desperate to hold them there. 'I have things to tell you, things you should know.' She hung onto the car door, preventing Frances from shutting it. From leaving her. She felt, rather than saw, Nathan suck in his cheeks and chew the inside of his bottom lip, his eyes fixed on Holly. She understood his confusion. Who could blame him?

She searched for the clincher, the thing that would keep them there. But she came up empty-handed. She had nothing. Nathan had heard enough. He turned the key in the ignition and turned away from her, looking behind him to check for oncoming traffic.

'Sorry,' Frances repeated, third time lucky, then she pulled the car door out of Holly's grasp and shut it.

Nathan started pulling away from the kerb, away from Holly. Through the glass of the passenger-side window, Holly yelled at Frances. 'Why don't you love her?' she yelled, emotion breaking her words apart as they left her mouth. She'd meant to say, *You need to love her*, but the other had come out instinctively. She pointed behind her towards the hospital. 'She's in there, waiting for you to love her. To take care of her.'

If it hadn't been awkward initially, which it had, it was definitely awkward now. Frances kept her eyes focused straight ahead, through the windscreen, looking at the road, pretending Holly wasn't on the other side of the glass yelling at her.

'She needs a father,' she cried out, as Nathan made the break and entered the stream of traffic. 'She deserves to be loved. By both of you. Please.'

His tail-lights flared as he reached the intersection, then extinguished as he turned the corner. Away from her.

And that, right there, taken from the point of view of changing one's future for the better, would have to be considered a fail.

6.13 pm

The dad was cooking spaghetti bolognaise. Sauce out of a tin.

Everything Frances had ever told her about her father was a lie. He hadn't died in a skiing accident. He was here, alive, in Los Angeles, right now. And the two of them were together. Why had Frances lied? And such an enormous lie, too? At least if she'd known her dad was alive, Holly could have written to him. Could have had some kind of relationship with him.

And to top it all off, she was about to eat spaghetti with tinned bolognaise sauce – exactly the same as last night. There was only so much one person could stand in a single day.

'We had this last night,' Holly said.

'Makes sense,' the dad said, keeping it light. 'It's a family favourite. How can they squeeze so much deliciousness into one can?'

'Not wanting to state the obvious, but that's two nights in a row,' Holly said, her words thin and jagged, their edges sharp, like they, too, had been taken to with a can opener.

The dad looked as if he wasn't sure where to go with that, so opted to say nothing. This small kitchen with its two-burner cooktop and processed spaghetti sauce was so angry-making. Holly didn't want it, any of it. And especially not bolognaise from a tin.

'Well, I love it,' said Loolah, defending her dad. Like Holly was rubbing his nose in the fact that he didn't live with them anymore. 'I could have it every single night and be happy,' she announced.

'Well, you would, wouldn't you,' Holly said, turning her can-opener-sharp words on Loolah. Loolah, sitting there so smug, like everything was right with the world, when it so clearly wasn't.

'Trinity!' the dad said, the severity in his voice reining her in.

And then, as suddenly as Holly's rage had flared, it evaporated. This wasn't about spaghetti sauce in a can. It was about Nathan and Frances. It was about Frances's lies, all those years, every year of her life, lied to.

'I'm sorry,' she said, her shoulders slumping. 'It wasn't a good day today.' She only realised once the words were out of her mouth that they'd subconsciously mirrored what Frances had said to her earlier.

The dad put his arm around her shoulders and dragged her in close to him, his spoon still doing the rounds of the saucepan, keeping the sauce from sticking and burning.

'You doing okay?' he asked.

'Yeah.'

'Well, don't take it out on us,' Loolah said huffily.

Holly grinned at the indignant little face staring up at her from the table.

'I'm sorry,' she said.

'Apology accepted,' Loolah said, the formality of the words contrasting with the messiness of her hair, the dirt smear across her face, the shortness and sweetness of her.

'Thank you,' said Holly.

'Don't let it happen again,' said Loolah.

Holly laughed.

And just like that, family made her feel better.

9.41 pm

Holly sat cross-legged on her bed, the Los Angeles telephone directory spread open in front of her on the quilt. There were pages of Kings – thousands, probably tens of thousands, maybe even hundreds of thousands of them in the greater Los Angeles area. It was an impossible task. She groaned. All those Kings were mocking her from the tightly typed, tissue-thin pages, hiding the one King she needed to speak with.

She walked over to the desk and placed her fingers on Brother Orange. The keys felt strangely warm, like someone else's hands had just been there. She needed to talk to someone about her day, and Trinity was the only person who'd understand.

You're, she typed. She'd planned on *You're the only person who knows how I feel*, but You're was as far as she got.

You're wanting me to stay home? Hah! No way. I've been far too busy ruining your life. And let me tell you, today was a good one! Drove to school, maaaybe sideswiped a few cars. Only a bit of damage, but no fatalities, so that's a good day, right? Reaction to your hair: classic! People literally stopped in the hallway to stare as I walked past. Or maybe it was the clothes I was wearing? These old overalls I found in the hall cupboard. Couldn't find anything decent in your CRAPPED OUT wardrobe with all the RIPPED UP clothes. Oh and I gave all your classes the day off. Aiming for Teacher of the Year.

One interesting thing – I went to the library so I could find an encyclopaedia to look up time travel, soul swapping, whatever it is you've done to me, but then the librarian showed me the computer and look at me go. I could look up anything. I mean, don't get me wrong, I still plan to DESTROY you, but the internet is pretty cool. I searched for myself in there, but couldn't find me. What does that MEAN? What have you DONE? By the way, in good news, I found your credit card in your tote. I've bought a plane ticket to LA for Monday and when I get there I'm gonna HUNT YOU DOWN. You've got five days to swap us back. The clock is a-tickin'. You've been warned.

And then silence.

Holly pulled the page out of the typewriter and re-read the words. Bloody Trinity. This wasn't what Holly needed to read after the day she'd had. Furious, she rolled in a fresh piece of paper, ready to type a reply, but there was a knock on the bedroom door, throwing Holly out of the zone.

'Hon,' the mom said, coming into the room.

Holly instinctively ripped the page out of the rogue typewriter in case Trinity started typing from the future again; rested her arm on the keys to make sure no words could be typed.

'It's getting late,' the mom said. 'Loolah's in bed, and do you mind?' Meaning, *Do you mind not typing because no one's getting any sleep with that racket going on.*

But Holly needed to write back. 'Yeah, of course. Sorry,' she said, trying to remain calm. 'I just have one last small thing to write, and then I'm done. One tiny sentence. Is that okay?'

'Sure.' The mom came over and kissed the top of Holly's head, then looked her square in the eyes, like she was about to say something. Instead, she lightly touched Holly's cheek, then turned and left the room.

Holly put in a piece of paper.

Trinity. You need to get a grip. I'll write to you tomorrow, but you need to stop blaming me. When will you realise none of this is my fault? I'm trying to fix things here. And maybe stop and think. It's pointless for you to fly to America because I'm here in 1980, not 2020.

No point mincing words.

Holly whipped out the page and tossed a jumper over the keys to stop any further communication. She wasn't sure if that would help, but it was the best she could come up with at short notice.

3.24 am

Holly woke up to a person crawling into bed alongside her.

For a moment her body softened, thinking it was Jamie, but then she remembered she wasn't with Jamie anymore. She was with Michael. And then she stiffened, because this person was a completely different shape and size from Michael, and hang on, this wasn't her bed, this was Trinity's bed. The voice of the other person, soft and whispery, said, 'I had a nightmare.'

Loolah.

Holly settled back against her pillow and opened her arms, folding them around the little body, feeling the fresh-out-of-bed warmth as she held Loolah close. 'You're okay, shh, you're okay,' she whispered into Loolah's ear. Same as the mom had said to her only a few hours ago when they were looking down at baby Holly.

'I dreamt someone was in their car, watching the house,' Loolah said, her voice getting sleepier now she knew she was safe with her sister. 'And I was trying to call out, but no one could hear me, and...' but even as she was saying the words she was drifting back to sleep, taking Holly with her.

Day 6
WEDNESDAY,
5 MARCH
1980

7.32 am

Holly half-heartedly ferried cereal from her bowl to her mouth. She felt tired and unsettled. She had to find Frances and Nathan, but all those Kings in the phone book... Even if she assumed that Nathan lived on his own and went straight to the N Kings, it would take weeks to ring through all the columns. She wanted to stay home from school today and start making calls, but presuming he had some kind of job, he wouldn't even be there to pick up the phone. She could leave a message on his answering machine, but that was only *if* he had an answering machine. How many people even *had* answering machines in 1980? Were they common or rare? Dime a dozen or seriously fancy? Besides, how could she say what she needed to say in a message on a machine?

If only she could ask Trinity's mom to get the forwarding address out of the hospital files – surely Frances would have had to give details of where she was staying. It would be much quicker and guaranteed to have all the details correct, but there was no way she'd be able to convince the mom to do that.

Lewis leant against the kitchen bench, eating his cereal. He reached into his schoolbag and pulled out a couple of sheets of glossy photographic paper as he chewed, then pushed them towards her. 'Thought you might want to take a look at some of the shots from last week,' he said, the proof sheets on the counter between them. 'I developed them yesterday. I'm booked into the darkroom at lunchtime today to develop the other roll, and then that's all of them done.'

Tiny black-and-white photos ran the length of each sheet, sprocket holes along the edges of each strip of film. Each tiny photo a close-up of the neck and mouth of a girl: Trinity.

She'd stood against the blank white wall of his bedroom, angling her head, pouting, sticking out her tongue playfully, running it over her lips, flirting with the camera, trying to make her neck look as long and appealing as possible. Her palms pressed against the cool plaster as, eyes closed, she tilted her head back and rested against the wall. She opened her eyes and stared up at the ceiling, then dipped her chin and looked down the barrel of the camera at him. He straightened slightly so he was no longer looking through the camera lens, instead looking over it, straight at her. And then she laughed and said, 'Bite me,' and the moment shattered, like a bowl filled with Frosted Flakes.

Holly felt a surge of guilt for spying on such a personal memory of Trinity's.

'There are some good ones in here,' he was saying, 'but I think there'll be some better ones in the next roll. The light was better.'

Unbidden, a poem popped into Holly's head.

Here's my neck, feel free to bite
It's early yet, we got all night
Just dip your mouth under my chin
Your teeth are sharp, it's not a sin
Now here's a scar, well lah-di-dah
You don't own me, you're not my tsar.

I'm not some victim drained and blue
The tables turned and I own you
Or maybe not, I can't tell yet
But next black night, I'll cash my debt

She flicked a glance at him from under her eyelashes. Again with that handsome face of his. Except she shouldn't be thinking of him in that way. Even if the bodies were the same age, the souls weren't.

She focused back on the images. As an art teacher, she knew they were great. The lighting, the composition – Lewis knew what he was doing. She pincered her fingers over one of the frames, absent-mindedly trying to enlarge it as though it was on the screen of her phone.

Lewis frowned at her. 'What are you doing?'

Holly jumped, realising her mistake. How did you explain something that had no precedent? Technology that wouldn't be introduced for decades to come? She rubbed her fingers together, stalling for time, and then finally said, 'I…there was a piece of, like, a hair or something on it.' And she repeated the motion once more to prove it. Nothing suspicious to see here.

'Okay, well, anyway,' Lewis went on, 'I wouldn't mind you having a look at the rest of the shots. Can you be bothered meeting me in the art room at lunchtime? Give me a victim's perspective?' He smiled at her.

The art room. The one place in this strange world that she'd be completely at home. She could picture it. There'd be lots of natural light, windows running along one wall, paint-spattered tables. 'Sounds good,' she said, hauling her nylon Pan Am bag onto her shoulder. 'I'll be interested to see them.'

Lewis picked up his bag and joined her, but as they were walking out the door, he frowned. 'Where's your guitar?'

Holly looked at him. 'Um. Upstairs?'

'Don't you have lessons on a Wednesday?'

'Oh yeah.' Did she? She didn't know.

'Do you want me to come upstairs and brush your teeth for you, too?' he asked.

'No. Why? What do you mean?'

'Well, seems I have to remember everything else for you.'

He was joking, but the intimacy of him standing in front of her, leaning over, brushing her teeth... she could picture it. Holly quickly headed upstairs.

She needed to find Nathan King and get out of this life. Fast.

8.24 am

Maths. Math. O'Farrell.

Holly went up to him, took out her page of incomplete homework and put it on the table beside him. 'I hadn't done it Monday,' she said without prompting. 'As you probably guessed.'

O'Farrell looked at her poker-faced, but the hint of a smile played on his mouth. 'You surprise me,' he said. No, she didn't. Not even a bit.

'Anyway,' she went on, 'I tried to do it, but most of it I wasn't able to finish. In fact, to be honest, most of it I couldn't even start. But at least, in good news, I'm handing something in.'

O'Farrell glanced down at the page, then looked back up at her. 'You're a smart girl, Legs,' he said. 'All you need to do is pay a bit of attention. Do the homework each night, bare minimum. It's not that hard.'

'You shouldn't call me Legs,' Holly said.

'Okay, what about this – I don't call you Legs, you pay a bit more attention in class. How's that sound?'

'Deal.' She wondered if they should shake on it, but decided against it. She turned to go back to her desk.

'You know I take extra math in the library at lunch on Mondays,' O'Farrell said. 'I could catch you up. It wouldn't take you long to get up to speed.'

Holly considered his proposal. And then she said, 'Yeah. Okay. I will.'

He looked surprised. 'Really?'

'Yeah.'

'Trinity?' he said.

'What?'

'Nothing. Just checking it's you in there.'

Holly laughed. He didn't know the half of it.

There you go, Trinity: catch-up maths classes. You wreck my life, I'll wreck yours.

10.17 am

Holly sat listening to the discussion about what sort of an impact Vienna would have had on Asher Lev if he'd gone there that first time with his father. Even though she hadn't read the book, the whole exercise seemed eerily relevant to her – the idea that if you changed one thing, you would change an entire life.

Exactly.

She put up her hand to make the point. Waited. Other kids were called on to make comments. The Reaper wrote some on the blackboard. Holly's arm was getting tired.

'Jacob,' the Grim Reaper said, looking through Holly like she was made of thin air to call on someone who didn't even have their hand up.

Classic avoidance. The Grim Reaper would choose every other person in the class before she asked Holly – only interested in singling her out if she was unprepared.

Holly went to put her hand back down. She wasn't even sure what she wanted to say anymore, and besides, if the Reaper wasn't going to ask her, what was the point? But then something in her body resisted – something in her very bones fired up with defiance. Call it the Trinity factor. And instead of putting her hand down, she put her other hand up to support the weight of her arm. She kept it propped there for the rest of the class. When the bell rang, she felt what could only be described as a sense of satisfaction that Mrs Grimwade had never pointed to her at all.

1.03 pm

The art room was everything Holly had known it would be, and more. The smell of it, the paint; the evidence of industry strewn across tables, the floor, every surface. She took in the messiness of it, the spirit of creativity. She wanted to get her hands dirty, grab herself a piece of paper and start sketching, suddenly longing for her own life. She missed teaching art, making art.

Lewis was standing at one of the long tables, his hands either side of a piece of paper in front of him. Holly walked over and stared down at it with him.

It was one of the black-and-white photos from the proof sheet, Trinity's face enlarged to almost A3 size. Her neck was arched, her mouth slightly open. Two small punctures had been drawn in by hand, mimicking a bite, a line of red ink running from the puncture marks and pooling in the brightly coloured chocolate wrappers that Lewis had pasted to her neck. The wrappers in question were from Baby Ruth candy bars, the red and white of the wrappers working tonally against the cream skin of Trinity's neck, the red of her hand-painted mouth, the trickle of blood. The wrappers were folded down, exactly as you'd do with any bar you were eating, but the way he'd arranged it, it mimicked one of those Elizabethan lace collars.

The sense being that she was a piece of candy, unwrapped.

On the table were other wrappers Lewis was collaging together to use on other photos: Tootsie Rolls, Chick-O-Sticks, Mary Janes, all confectionary that Holly had never heard of until now, all of them with female names.

It wasn't just the skill and craft that impressed Holly, but the way Lewis carried through an idea. How original, conceptual, the work was. 'This is genius,' she said to him.

He didn't answer; it was almost like he hadn't heard her, but she knew he had, because there were only the two of them in the room, and she'd said it out loud. Also, a blush rose from his neck – a blush tonally suited to the Baby Ruth candy bars. To the drops of blood. To Trinity's open mouth.

Holly needed to stop thinking of him this way. But was it in fact her thinking this way, or Trinity?

'And I wanted to show you these as well.' He led her to the bench that ran along the back wall, where three small canvases were propped up, popping with psychedelic hues. 'I've done these for Susie Sioux's birthday party next weekend,' he said.

They were oversized tarot cards. One featured a man painted, bare-chested, sitting on a throne, a goat head on his shoulders. Magazine cutouts of people drinking and dancing were collaged along the base. The second canvas was of a priestess holding a sword in one hand and a rose in the other, again with a party-scene collage running along the base. The third had an angel, wings extended, looking over another collaged party crowd.

'You think she'll like them?' he asked, a charming vulnerability underpinning the question.

The brushstrokes, the confidence of the lines, the collage effect, the way Lewis had used the space on each page – he was a genuine talent. Holly looked over at him, his arms folded across his body.

'These are amazing,' she finally said.

He shrugged. 'They're not bad.'

'No. You're being modest. They're really good.' But something nagged at her. She knew those lines. The use of collage, the style. 'Hang on,' she said, clicking her fingers at him. 'Lewis Rodda.' She'd studied his work when she was at art school. But Lewis's last name wasn't Rodda. It was Webster.

'What?'

'You're Lewis Rodda.'

'Why would you say that?' he said slowly.

She paused, trying to think of the right answer. And then she just shrugged. 'I don't know.'

He looked at her very strangely. Finally he said, 'Rodda is my mum's maiden name. I've been thinking I don't really want to use Webster anymore, because I haven't seen the old man in years, and obviously I don't want to go with Sinclair, because that's Rob's name. But it's so weird that you would say that, because you couldn't possibly know.'

He was right. There was no way she could have known he was thinking of changing his name to Rodda.

'Lucky guess, I s'pose,' she said limply.

'Trinity. There's no way you could have guessed that. Ever since last weekend, half the time I feel like I don't even know you. But then I look again, and it's you. I can't explain it, but you're different. You're you, but you're not you.'

Holly didn't answer for a long time. And then finally she said, 'I think I've got concussion.'

'You don't have concussion.'

'I do.'

'You don't.'

'What, you're a doctor now?'

'No. And you don't have concussion.'

Holly chewed on her bottom lip, wondering what to say next. Could she actually tell him stuff? Tell him what had really happened?

'Last weekend,' she finally said. 'After I woke up on the footpath. I keep…it's like I kind of…this is going to sound ridiculous, but I can sometimes see little snippets of the future. But not my future, someone else's. I know it sounds unbelievable, but I don't know what else to say. I know it doesn't make sense.'

She could hear her voice getting shaky. She didn't want to tell him everything – there was no way she could share all that. Even sharing this much was threatening to overwhelm her.

'There was a crack,' Lewis said after a pause. 'Not like thunder. Like a literal crack. Like a plate breaking. An enormous plate. At first I thought it was an earthquake. That was what made me come out of my house. And when I came out, and you were lying on the footpath out the front, with that guy trying to put you in his car, there was a kind of shimmering haze around you. Which doesn't make sense either.'

Holly looked up at Lewis. She thought of watching him eat his cereal every morning. Walking to school together. Him complaining that she always made him late. So handsome. And lovely. And tall. Plus, he smelt good.

He looked down at her.

It was a definite moment – a moment between the two of them, because he'd heard her, believed her. But, no, it wasn't. It was actually a moment between him and Trinity, which Holly shouldn't be there for.

He reached out and took hold of her hand.

Holly drew her hand back and pushed her hair behind her ear. 'Anyway, I have to go,' she said. Fake-bright. 'I have, you know, classes to go to. These are great.' She tapped one of his oversized tarot canvases as she turned to leave. 'She's gonna love them.'

'Trinity,' he said, a frown cleaving two lines between his eyebrows.

'Honestly, I have to go.' She walked out of the art room and didn't look back.

2.31 pm

Mr Clavis was the guitar teacher.

Holly hadn't realised until this moment how much the guitar took her away from her thoughts. The music echoed inside her chest while at the same time filtering through her ears into the very core of her being. Her sense of touch was busy with the strings, her sight focused on the music sheet in front of her. The smell of the resin filled the music room. The taste of each note soaked into her tongue.

All five senses, occupied.

This girl. This guitar. Truly a joy to spend time with.

3.16 pm

'Lewis said you had a look at his photos at lunchtime?' Aprilmayjune said as they trundled along the footpath towards her house, schoolbags hoicked onto their shoulders. 'What did you think of them? And the canvases he's going to give to Susie Sioux – pretty cool, huh? She's gonna love them.'

Holly didn't want to think about Lewis. What was she supposed to do? Kiss the guy? It would be all kinds of wrong. Or would it? She was this person, Trinity, living this life. That was who he'd been moving towards. Maybe it was okay to kiss the boy? She really didn't know, and she really didn't want to think about it.

'Yeah,' she said. 'They're great.' Conversation closed. Moving on.

'I mean, when I looked at them, the photos...' April continued. 'What's going on with you two?'

Holly flicked a guilty look at her. 'Nothing. Why?'

'Come on. They're like sex on a stick.'

'They're photos of my neck.'

'*Tech*nically,' April said, clearly not believing her at all. And Holly understood why. She'd seen the photos. The sexiness of them was right there for anyone to see. 'But come on, tell me there's nothing between you guys.'

'There's nothing.'

'Yeah, but there is.'

'He's just a friend.'

'You've always said that,' April said. 'But the past few weeks? Something's changed.'

'Nothing's changed.'

April slid a sceptical look over at her friend. Holly looked away.

Nothing to see here.

3.29 pm

April's house had a massive fuck-off front fence, behind which hid a huge front yard, where there was a big old oak tree, the one Holly and April and Sooz had spent many, many days climbing and sitting in and swinging from when they were kids.

Not Holly. Trinity.

There was an enormous pool in the backyard, where they'd spent just as many days. A tennis court. In-built trampoline. This house was almost as familiar as her own. April's dad was some kind of plastic surgeon, and when you were a plastic surgeon in LA, that meant a fuck-off front fence, tennis court, pool, trampoline, and all the rest of it.

On the front doorstep, along with a waiting Susie Sioux and Heather, was a single roll of toilet paper. April leant down and picked it up, then unfurled the first couple of sheets to reveal a handwritten note on the tissue-thin squares. Her face fell as she read it.

'What is it?' Susie Sioux asked.

April didn't say anything for a moment, then started reading out loud.

'*Dear April*,' she said, her voice not betraying any emotions. '*Consider this my official break-up letter. Written on toilet paper, because I think it's appropriate. You've treated me like shit these past few weeks, so it's only reasonable. Feel free to use the rest of this roll in the way it was originally intended. Carl.*'

Holly looked over at April, trying to gauge her feelings. She was offended on April's behalf. But on the other hand… *Good for you, Carl. Don't take shit from anyone.* The fact that April had been considering breaking up with him because he'd had his hair cut – well, really, she couldn't be too devastated about it. 'Are you okay?' Holly asked, putting her hand on April's arm.

'That's awful,' Susie Sioux said.

'What an asshole,' agreed Heather.

'I mean, seriously,' Susie Sioux went on, 'dumped via toilet roll…' But then she didn't say anything further, her hand up to her mouth as she tried to smother the laugh that was spilling through her fingers. 'I'm sorry, April, but it's just that…' And then more laughter, which triggered Heather, and rippled over to Holly despite herself, before finally even April started laughing too. Tears rolled down all of their faces, none of them able to speak from sheer, unbridled, breathless laughter.

'I almost want to get back with him now,' April decided when they'd finally managed to regain their composure. 'Except he's still got that bad haircut.' Setting them all off all over again.

5.14 pm

Holly walked down the driveway of her house, past Trinity's mom's car. She could feel something at her back, that prickling sensation you got when someone was looking at you. She turned around just as a long white boaty American car sped past and drove down the street away from her.

5.16 pm

Holly walked upstairs to her bedroom and took the sweater off the typewriter. She could feel the heat radiating off the keys – there'd be a letter in there from Trinity, she was sure of it.

She rolled in a piece of paper.

Hope

She got one word out, the start of *Hope you're okay, I've got so much to tell you*, before the typewriter exploded.

Hope you don't mind but I've just dumped your boyfriend. This is how it went.

Him (turning up on front porch): Hi.

Me: What?

Him: You okay?

Me: No.

Him: (something boring, can't remember what).

Me: goodbye (going to shut the door).

Him: Wait. What's going on?

Me: I'm flying to LA on Monday. Have a good life.

Him: (something else boring, can't remember, wasn't paying attention).

Me: Shutting door in his face.

Just checking off boxes. By the way, I mean seriously, what a dweeb. Even YOU could do better than him, and that's saying something. Oh. Also. The head of art wants to have a meeting with you tomorrow. Something about not being happy with the way you're behaving at the moment. I mean, sure, maybe you don't know how to swap us back, or maybe you do. I'm just saying, if I was you, I'd get this show on the road.

Holly stared down at the page. It was the injustice of it all that got to her. She had been trying so hard, even though it was like she was treading water and liable to sink at any moment. She was exhausted. She'd messed things up at the hospital with Frances and Nathan; she couldn't possibly go through all the Kings in the telephone book and find him, there was no way; and now Trinity had dumped Michael and it seemed Holly might not have a job by the time they swapped back.

Holly angrily scrolled a fresh piece of paper into the typewriter and started banging words up onto the page.

You know what, Trinity, she jabbed at the typewriter keys, if I could get out of your life, I would. It's not like your life is so perfect. You don't need to go getting all...

She searched for the right word, but couldn't find it.

...whatever with me. We're both struggling. If you think I'm happy living your stupid life, you'd be wrong.

But then she stopped typing. The truth was, she *was* happy here. The mom was downstairs, getting dinner organised. Loolah was sitting on the couch watching *The Brady Bunch*, the volume turned up to maximum. Driving lessons with the dad. Susie Sioux. Aprilmayjune. Heather. Lewis.

Her life in the future was filled with empty holes. Grannie Aileen had died. Zoe had died. Frances had died. Evie was still around, but she was busy with her husband and her kids. Michael was... Trinity was right. He was a dweeb.

She compared that to what she experienced here. This was a life that she had to approach at full tilt. Guitar, friends, family, running, softball, even shoplifting, even hitchhiking – Trinity had grown up knowing that she was safe, that she could be unafraid, that life was worth living. She was free to make mistakes, because her life didn't depend on getting everything right; her mom and her dad and her sister and her friends would all love her and take care of her no matter what.

The red-hot anger melted away. Trinity was just living a Trinity-type life, but in a Holly setting. She was stirring things up, messing around, not caring too much. Holly had to admire that. She thought about yesterday afternoon with Frances and Nathan. Trinity probably would have handled it better than Holly had. Something about Trinity would have made them stay and listen.

All this time, Holly had been acting like she should be taking control since she was the adult here, but now she realised she was wrong. Trinity had a different way of approaching things – one that worked better sometimes. They should be working together. Holly put her hands back over the keys and started typing again, more slowly, less enraged.

I'm sorry, I'm all over the shop. I saw my parents yesterday. Frances and Nathan.

Something in her chest jolted at putting those two names together.

You already know some of this, but other stuff I haven't caught you up on yet. I was born at St Anne's. Your mom was there – she helped deliver me. You and I, we're both born ten weeks prem. Both Rhnull. Both broke our collarbones, even. I went to St Anne's yesterday and donated blood. To myself. It blew my mind. And while I was there I saw my mom,

Oh. That was weird. She'd automatically put 'mom' instead of 'mum'.

Frances, with my dad, Nathan. All my life I've been told he died before I was born, but there he was. Both of them, together. So everything I've ever been told is a lie. I think that's why we've swapped: so I can fix things and have a better life second time around.

It's not about you. It's me.

But when I saw them yesterday, I messed up. I didn't fix anything. I need to find them, go talk to them again. But I don't know where they are. And I don't think I can find them on my own.

You're there in the future, with my laptop and the internet and everything that makes finding people so much easier. All I've got here is the phone directory with thousands and thousands of Kings to trawl through. So I was thinking maybe you could look up Nathan King on the internet? If you could get in touch with him, you could ask him what his address was in 1980. Even a suburb would help. If you say you're a friend of Frances Fitzgerald, he should get back to you.

By the way, you're right: Michael is a dweeb.

Also, your life? It's pretty perfect.

From Holly

8.47 pm

The typewriter remained silent all night.

Holly had eaten dinner in her room after telling the mom she had too much homework to do. She'd played her guitar, read some Asher Lev, even attempted some math. But the typewriter's keys stayed cool and quiet — there wasn't another letter in there yet.

It was as she heard Loolah getting ready for bed, brushing her teeth in the bathroom, that Holly sensed a change in the typewriter. She went over and looked down at it. She was starting to get the hang of this. It seemed that all she needed to do was type a single something, and that would set Trinity off.

She took a punt. Tapped at the letter 'I'.

Trinity took over from there.

I don't care about your mom and dad, whether he's alive or not. I want to be home, in my bedroom, back with my mom and my dad and Loolah and Susie Sioux and April and Lewis and Heather and all my friends and going to school like I'm supposed to.

I can't remember what number my locker is at school. I can't remember the name of our neighbors (not Lewis's family, obviously, but the other side). I'm starting to forget things.

But then there's a photo on your bookshelf of you and Zoe and Evie. Zoe reminds me so much of Susie Sioux – they don't look the same, but there's something about her. Have you noticed? And the weird thing is, I remember when that photo was taken. You were in Bali. You were sitting at this bar that was cut into a cliff and just after the photo was taken this enormous wave came and drenched you all and washed your drinks off the table and you couldn't stop laughing, and I remember all of it, even though I wasn't there.

I'm frightened that I'm starting to remember your life more clearly than mine. I just want to come home. So I'm getting on your computer right now. I'm not leaving this house until I find Nathan King. And when I do, I'll let you know.

'Hon?' the mom stood in her doorway.

The typewriter was still, but Holly rested her arm on it just in case. 'It's okay, I've finished,' she said.

The mom came over and gave her a kiss goodnight. Smiled. Patted her hair. 'Night, sweet pea,' she said.

'Night...Mom,' Holly replied.

For the first time, it felt right.

Day 7

THURSDAY, 6 MARCH 1980

7.12 am

Holly had a dream that lagged into her first waking moments. She'd been walking through the corridors of St Luke's. Except she wasn't Holly inside, she was Trinity – young, sixteen years old, walking the halls with the other teachers and passing students in their uniforms. Her hair was chopped short, and she was wearing a pair of paint-spattered canvas runners on her feet that matched her paint-spattered overalls.

When Holly woke up, she knew how Trinity could quickly and simply find Nathan's 1980 address. She pushed a fresh sheet of paper into Brother Orange's carriage.

In the hallway cupboard, where you got my overalls from, is a box. It's brown leather, on the top shelf. Inside, you'll find a photo of Frances and Nathan together in Morocco. Under the photo are a couple of letters written to my mum from Nathan, while she was travelling around Europe. One of the letters, I'm pretty sure, has his LA address. This is it, Trinity! If you send me the address, I can go see him. He holds the key to us swapping back, I'm sure of it.

She sat back in her chair and re-read what she'd typed. This was it. She was going home. As soon as Trinity sent her through the address, they'd be swapping back.

Holly thought about Susie Sioux and Aprilmayjune and Heather and Lewis and all her friends at school. The mom, the dad, Loolah. She was going to miss them. She could feel everything coming to an end.

Today might very well be her very last day in 1980. Forever.

7.48 am

There was an awkwardness between Holly and Lewis as they walked to school together – an uncomfortable something that had its roots in yesterday's art room situation.

As they walked along the footpath, Holly's new Lotus Strat banged against her leg. Lewis reached over and took it out of her hand.

'It's fine,' she said. 'I can carry it.'

He ignored her and shifted it over to his other hand, away from her. She wondered whether to feel insulted or glad. It was heavy, so she was glad, but on the other hand, he was implying that he was stronger than her, which was insulting. But also correct. She decided, on balance, to be glad she didn't have to carry it all the way to school. Not that she would ever tell him that.

'So you've got rehearsals round at Susie Sioux's tonight?' Lewis finally said. 'For the party?' There was a hollow tone to his question, as if he didn't really care.

The thing was, he already knew the answer. He'd been the one to remind her to grab her guitar before they left the house (again), and when she'd brought down her acoustic guitar, he'd said she needed her electric. He was just making mindless conversation, acting like everything was fine between them when it wasn't.

He'd taken hold of her hand in the art room and she'd taken it back. He'd received the message, loud and clear.

Except he was wrong about the message. If she could have, she would have given him her other hand too.

12.15 pm

Softball training felt good. It was a relief to slip into neutral and not think.

Before Holly had come to training she'd been mulling over what Trinity had said in her letter about having forgotten her locker number and not being able to remember the name of the neighbours. Holly was noticing the same thing. She still couldn't remember the game Grannie Aileen had played with her girlfriends every Thursday. She was almost certain it was mahjong, but it could have been bridge. She couldn't say for sure. She niggled at her other memories like a kid with a loose tooth. Evie's children were Hope and ... something beginning with 'M'. Marcia. Marcie? The students in her classes: Bianca and ... Luce. Tildy. Leila. Audrey. Della. But there were others, names just out of reach – maybe ... no, she was coming up blank.

But she didn't need to think about any of that during training. Softball was purely about catch and throw, run and slide. Her job was to reach up and catch the high balls when they came to her; pitch the ball into the target of the other girls' gloves.

It felt like hope and joy, and even a little bit like mercy.

And then she remembered: Mercy. Evie's eldest was called Mercy.

3.52 pm

Holly, April and Susie Sioux walked through the front gate into Susie Sioux's front yard. A grove of camellias stood on one side of a shallow pond, and a single perfect maple next to the wooden double front doors was starting to shoot fresh green leaves.

The three of them took off their shoes and left them arranged at the front door, then walked barefoot down the corridor towards the kitchen at the back of the house. The seagrass matting felt pleasantly scratchy under Holly's feet. The kitchen had plain wooden slatted cupboard doors, and a large pot bubbled away on the stove. There was a sense of serenity and calm over the entire place. They grabbed some snacks out of the pantry and continued into the back room, which had sliding glass doors looking out over the long backyard, where cherry blossoms were starting to bud. Over in the corner, April's drum kit was already set up.

'But I don't play anything,' April had said when Trinity and Susie Sioux proposed starting a band. 'And I can't sing.'

'What about drums? You just bang at 'em,' Susie Sioux suggested.

'Well, what does leave me with?' Heather said. 'Triangle?'

Susie Sioux had laughed. Unimpressed, Heather had refused to even consider joining their band.

Holly squatted down on the floor, unclipped her guitar case and took out her new Lotus. She plugged it in, then hoisted the strap over her head and arranged her shoulders, feeling the comfortable weight.

'Nice,' Susie Sioux said.

Holly smiled down at her guitar. 'Yeah, she's a beauty.'

She wondered how much longer she was going to be here, in this place. She was really going to miss these girls. Even thinking about not seeing them, especially Susie Sioux with her Zoe energy, pained her heart.

Susie Sioux fiddled with her bass guitar, the size of it swamping her small frame. Her choppy black hair fell over her pale face, her fringe cut so long and so sharp it threatened to slice off her eyelashes. A cigarette dangled from her red lips.

The three of them had been standing in their favourite record store on Beeswitch Street when the tinny Japanese opening riff of 'Hong Kong Garden' by Siouxsie and the Banshees spilled through the speakers. They stared at each other, wide-eyed, loving how cool it was. Two minutes and fifty-two seconds later, Susan Watanabe had found her inspiration. It was a pivotal hair-deciding, name-changing, lipstick-choosing moment. Back at her house, with Trinity and April in attendance, she cut a long blunt fringe into her black hair, layered on black eye make-up and smeared bright-red lipstick across her mouth. Welcome to the world, Susie Sioux.

April was not immune to the influence of female rock gods either. Her hair could have come straight off the head of Cherie Currie on the front cover of the *Runaways* album.

And Holly herself had black tips dyed in homage to Debbie Harry.

The three of them had crowded into the bathroom at Trinity's house, the pot plant precariously balanced on the edge of the bath. Her hair was loosely pulled into two pigtails, the tips sitting in two cups of black hair dye. Her shoulders ached from having to sit like that and not move until the dye took.

April flipped the drumsticks over her knuckles like some kind of rock'n'roll cheerleader, then fumbled them onto the ground. She looked up at Susie Sioux and Holly and grinned. 'Rock'n'roll!' she yelled, then picked her drumsticks back up and started banging at the drums, throwing her entire body into it. Though there wasn't much musical ability involved, Holly couldn't fault her energy. April stopped and looked over at Susie Sioux, who started playing something on her bass, the twang of it a reminder of something Holly couldn't quite put her finger on. Susie Sioux stopped and looked over at Holly, waiting for her musical reply.

Something in her body picked up the cue, and Holly found herself playing the same notes back to Susie Sioux on her Lotus. Then stopping.

Susie Sioux played some fresh notes.

Holly copied, her guitar giving the notes a different flavour.

Then Susie Sioux.

Then Holly.

April started hitting the drums, a simple rhythmic backdrop to both the guitars.

Then Susie Sioux.

Holly.

SusieSiouxHolly.

SusieSiouxHollyAprilmayjune.

SusieSiouxHollyAprilmayjuneSusieSiouxHolly
Aprilmayjune. The three of them slowly merging musically
until they were playing something that was part song,
part riffing, part singular vision.

And then, without anyone counting them in, without
Holly even realising it was happening, the three of them
were playing a song in perfect synchronicity. And then
another. And another. Song after song, a roll call of all-
female bands: the Bangles, the Runaways, the Go-Go's.

The volume was cranked up as loud as it would go
and Holly found herself enveloped by the music. New
pathways were being created in her brain, memories
being forged in this new world, the person called Holly
Fitzgerald becoming more and more abstract with each
passing chord. She ran her fingers over the steel strings,
a pleasant pain pressing into her calloused fingertips,
being here in this body, in this moment. Each lyric
she sang vibrated deep down in her core, making the
entire width and breadth of her skin fizz. Music echoed
from the speakers back in through her pores, creating a

feedback loop of sound and beauty and phosphorescence and forgetfulness.

Susie Sioux's mom came in to listen, holding a mandarin in her hand. Holly looked across the room at her, and her fingers stumbled on the fretboard. She lost her mojo as she experienced a flash of realisation. Susie Sioux's mom was a medium. She channelled spirits, flipped tarot cards, held séances, communed with the dead. That was what she did for a living. That was where the ouija board had come from. It was a part of Mrs Watanabe's kit. If anyone was going to pick Holly for a spiritual fraud, it was Susie Sioux's mom.

Holly felt trapped. Exposed. Her insides pulled taut like a steel string. She couldn't be caught. Not now. She was so close to fixing things. Besides, she was here to play music. To practise songs, timings, check levels, prep for Susie Sioux's party in a week's time. She needed to erect a wall emotionally, so that Mrs Susie Sioux couldn't see in.

Holly adjusted her shoulders, cricked her neck, turned back towards the microphone and went back to playing, armour back on, soul issue tamped down. She got so into character she didn't even notice when Mrs Watanabe left the room.

6.32 pm

April and Holly were putting on their shoes at the front door when they noticed Mrs Watanabe standing in the doorway. Running through her fingers was a black rosary. Her eyes were closed, and she swayed back and forth slightly. When she started speaking, it was in a vacant tone, like an automated message. 'The Date of Resetting is in motion,' she said.

Holly's cheeks instantly flushed hot, but in strange opposition there was the feeling of refrigerated water trickling down her spinal cord. Her heart was running away from her, but her legs were filled with sand.

Mrs Watanabe knew.

The Reset *was* in motion. Of all the babies born in Los Angeles on Friday, she'd found her little premmie baby-self in the humidicrib in St Anne's. She'd seen Frances and Nathan. Her dad was alive! What were the chances? Her own golden blood was in a bag in the fridge of the hospital, waiting for baby-her to need it. It felt like everything was about to click into place. Once Trinity sent through Nathan's address, Holly would go and visit her parents, sit down with them, talk to them, reset her entire future. The three of them a proper happy family. It was like a game of chess, set up, ready for the checkmate move.

Except then Mrs Watanabe said, 'When evil came to snatch her away, she was sent forty years into the future. But she's still in danger.'

Holly frowned. Shook her head slightly. That made no sense. Baby-her hadn't been sent forty years into the future. If anything, she'd been sent forty years into the past. And then the coin dropped into the slot machine, all the ducks lining up in a row. Mrs Watanabe wasn't talking about little baby-her in the hospital here; she was talking about Trinity. Forty years into the future.

'You've been sent to break the evil,' Mrs Watanabe intoned. 'Only when that happens will the Reset—'

Susie Sioux interrupted in irritation and embarrassment. 'God, Mom, what are you doing? You can't just turn up and start doing all your mumbo jumbo stuff out of the blue.' She pushed April and Holly out the door. 'April's dad's waiting out the front. Okay, bye, you guys. See ya.'

The door shut behind them before they could even respond.

'Whoa, that was weird,' April said as they walked down the front path, Holly's legs barely able to manage one foot in front of the other. 'I've never seen her mom do that before. Have you? It was kind of cool. And strange. What's the Date of Resetting? And who's forty years in the future?' April smacked Holly on the arm just before they got to her dad's car. 'Oh my god,' she said. 'Remember the séance on Sunday, Help Trinity Holly? Do you think that's got anything to do with this? Is that what she was talking about?'

Holly shook her head, not able to get the words out.

No, she wanted to say.

But yes. That's exactly what it was about.

Day 8

FRIDAY, 7 MARCH 1980

6.54 am

Holly had been awake for hours, mulling things over in her head. Why Trinity? She couldn't see anything – no offence to her – particularly amazing about the girl. She was an ordinary teenager failing at school. But Mrs Watanabe couldn't have been any clearer.

When evil came...she was sent forty years into the future...You've been sent to break the evil.

It was definitely Trinity who needed saving. Not baby-Holly.

Downstairs in the kitchen, Holly could hear Lewis chatting to Loolah. She padded over to the typewriter. She should write a letter. Tell Trinity what Mrs Watanabe had said. *Don't worry about getting me Nathan's address,* she would type. *It's not about me, it's you. You were thrown forty years into the future because you're in danger.*

But what made Trinity so special that the universe had intervened? Why her? Although Holly had to admit that there was a definite joy and light to being inside this body. She could feel it. She thought of the people who wanted to be friends with her. Of this life fully lived. Of the music that erupted from Trinity's body.

Even the Grim Reaper could sense it and was trying to douse the flame.

Still. No offence. Why Trinity?

And the other question was: Why Holly? Why send *her* back? Were they soul mates? Soul sisters? Family from a previous life? Why had she been chosen to break the evil?

If she was going to tell Trinity what was going on, she needed to get it straight in her own head first. She'd write to her this afternoon, as soon as she got home from school.

3.16 pm

Friday detention.

The day had passed in a kind of blur. Holly had felt as if she was barely there – more removed from things than she'd felt at any time since she'd woken up on the footpath last Friday. A week ago exactly. It was so strange to think of it. She'd been getting used to this life. Enjoying it.

She sat with her chin in her palm, staring down at the words *My Future* written across the top of her page, copied off the teacher's prompt on the blackboard. That was as much as she'd managed – two words scratched onto the page like a taunt. Because the fact was, her future had nothing to do with it: it was all about Trinity.

She couldn't say how long she sat like that – close to half an hour, perhaps – until suddenly her thoughts whipped into a furious anger and she started scribbling on the page.

In the future, my best friend will have died. There will be bushfires and a virus and chaos. Grannie Aileen has gone. I couldn't care less about Michael. I never did any of the things I set out to do. What's even the point of writing about the future when it's already done? Except it can be reset. And apparently it's up to me to reset it. Sure. La-di-dah. No worries! As if! Why me? What am I supposed to do? Why has this been dumped in my lap? And why her? Why the two of us together? How are we connected? And apart from all that, how am I supposed to break the evil? What does that even mean? It's—

'All right, students.' The teacher rose from the desk and gathered together the essays he'd been marking. 'That's time. Have a good weekend. Don't be here next Friday. I don't want to see any of your faces again.'

Holly stood up, grabbed the piece of paper she'd been writing on and walked up to the front of the class. 'Can I keep this?' she asked the teacher.

'Sure,' he said. 'You're more than welcome. I'm glad you found it useful.'

She hadn't found it useful. She just didn't want anyone else ever reading it. She stuffed it into the rubbish bin at the bottom of the stairs, then walked through the front doors of John Marshall High School and out onto the street beyond.

4.16 pm

Holly was nearly at her house when she sensed a car crawling along behind her.

She ignored it.

The car sped up, then pulled into the kerb a little way in front of her. Holly continued walking along the footpath, still ignoring it, safe in the knowledge that there was plenty of traffic around. She couldn't deny that the car seemed to be waiting especially for her, though. She clocked with a glance that it wasn't Trinity's dad – no blue GT stripe. She kept her eyes facing forward, but her peripheral vision continued scanning the car for clues: maybe was it one of the guys from school? Could be Mrs Glickman, even. It wasn't Trinity's mom, but it could be any number of other people. How would she know? There were so many things she still couldn't say for sure in this life. But as she walked past the car, she registered that there was something familiar about it. She knew it from somewhere. It was long and boaty, like every single other American car in 1980, but still...She tried to place it, rummaging around in her memories, and then she realised. She'd seen it the other day, out the front of the hospital. It was Nathan King's car. She glimpsed in through the passenger side window, and looking over at her from the driver's side wasn't a stranger. It was her father. The one man, out of all the thousands and thousands and thousands of people in the greater Los Angeles area, who she really wanted to talk to.

Her relief was immense.

'It's you,' she said to him, placing a hand on the windowframe.

'I thought that was you,' he said, pushing his cap back off his face. 'You had a lot to say the other afternoon. At the hospital,' he added.

She shook her head, trying to flick off the memory of how badly she'd handled it. 'I just wanted to talk,' she said.

'Sure. We can talk. But we're blocking traffic,' he said, then leant over and pushed open the passenger-side door for her. 'Get in.'

She hesitated for the merest moment. Obviously Holly wouldn't normally get in a car with a strange man, but this wasn't a stranger. This was her father. This was her chance to talk to him, to potentially change her entire life with this one conversation. Sure, she needed to break the evil for Trinity, but maybe she could do a little something for herself as well.

It went without saying that she got in.

'I don't have a lot of time,' he said. 'I'm picking someone up.' He glanced at his watch. 'We can talk on the way.'

In Trinity's bedroom, the keys on the orange typewriter started to burble like a pot simmering on the stove.

The beaten-up old Chevrolet had no seatbelts, which felt dangerous. What was it with the eighties? No bike helmets. No seatbelts. No safety. It was a manual, four on the floor, and Nathan drove faster than she'd have liked, cranking through the gears, the car lurching almost like an animal at every gear change. He was a man who enjoyed driving, being behind the wheel, she could tell.

Her dad.

He wasn't saying much. He had his window wound down, one hand on the steering wheel, the other resting on the gearshift between them. It took all her restraint not to bare-faced stare at him. After all these years of looking at a photograph, here he was, in person. His cap gave him that overall boyish look she knew so well, but up close he looked older than his, what, twenty-four years? Twenty-three? She tried to remember how old Frances had said he was when they'd first met.

'How old are you?' she asked, almost without meaning to. It seemed, as it came out of her mouth, such a personal question.

He slowed as he approached an intersection, crunched down from third to second gear.

'Why?' he asked.

'I'll guess,' she said, wanting to engage him in conversation. Wanting to be engaging. 'You're…twenty-four?'

He went back up to third. Shook his head imperceptibly.

'Higher or lower?'

'You're guessing. Not me.' Up to fourth.

'Lower.'

He shook his head.

'Higher then.'

Brainiac. He nodded.

'Okay. Twenty-five?'

He shook his head.

Asking the questions had the advantage of meaning she could turn and look at him more openly. His hair was shorter, had been cut since the photo had been taken. He was cleanly shaven now, instead of backpacker messy.

'Twenty-six?'

She could see what Frances would have seen in him. He was slightly brooding. The type of man whose thoughts you couldn't guess. The dimple in his cheek hadn't revealed itself yet, but that was because he wasn't smiling like he was in the photo. She wanted to make him smile. The dimple would feel like a reward.

'Twenty-seven?'

He nodded. A slight smile. Not enough to dimple.

'What about you?' he asked.

'What about me?'

'How old you?'

'Guess,' she said, wanting to keep the game going, but as the word came out of her mouth, she was swamped by the realisation of how strange it all was. He knew nothing about her. So why had he stopped to pick her up? Why had she got in the car with him?

'Sixteen?' he said.

She didn't answer, staring at him, trying to figure him out.

When he'd first stopped, why hadn't he simply got out of the car and talked to her there? He'd told her to get in because they were blocking traffic, but he could have just parked properly so he wasn't blocking the traffic. What was a twenty-seven-year-old man doing picking up a sixteen-year-old girl?

She shouldn't be here.

'Where are we going?' she asked, grappling around for some sense of what was going on, starting to feel 'yoi'.

'My parents just bought a new place,' he said. 'They arranged to meet the builder there this afternoon, but then my dad had to go back to work, so they asked for me to pick my mom up. Take her home.'

And just like that, yoi evaporated. He was picking up his mom. Exactly as you'd want a good, decent man to do. And then, like a domino knocking over its neighbour, the realisation tumbled into her brain.

His parents meant her grandparents. She hadn't even got so far as to think about them until now. Her entire focus had been on him, but of course he had parents. Brothers and sisters too, maybe – she didn't know. All of them connected to her. Family. A whole family she'd never known. And here she was.

'Your parents...' she said, and the words caught in her throat. 'They'll be there?'

He shrugged. 'My mom will be. Not my dad.'

She'd been putting her 2020 #metoo mindset onto this once-in-a-thousand-years situation. But these weren't normal circumstances. He'd picked her up because he knew, somehow, that they were connected. She was going to meet her grandma. This was a major reset.

And then another domino knocked into the shoulder of its neighbour.

Mrs Watanabe had been mid-prediction when Susie Sioux had interrupted her. Susie hadn't let her finish. Ever since Mrs Watanabe had stood at the door, the beads gently clicking as she worried the rosary through her fingers, Holly had been thinking, *Why Trinity? Why Trinity?* But now she realised the rest of the prediction, the other half. It wasn't just about Trinity. If Mrs Watanabe had been allowed to finish, she would have said it was about the both of them. Resetting both their lives.

A sense of quiet destiny fell over her.

She was exactly where she was supposed to be.

He turned the car into a quiet-looking street called Lowendover Avenue.

The two of them got out and walked side by side up to the second-last house before the avenue came to a dead end. The shadows cast by the trees wrapped around them. Holly looked through ornate wrought-iron gates that had seen better days, and up the driveway to the three storeys of a peeling Spanish-mission home that towered over them both. It was a beautiful old place. Like something a 1930s Hollywood movie star would have lived in. What was that movie? Sunset Boulevard. Like that.

'Is she here?' Holly asked, looking through the gate for his mom. Her grandma. She smiled to even think the word inside her head. Or maybe she'd prefer to be called Nana? It didn't matter. What mattered was seeing her, meeting her, talking to her. Resetting Holly's very own future. This was the key, she was sure of it.

'Looks like the builder's gone,' he said, pushing the gate open. 'She'll be up the back. Looking at the garden, probably. You want to come have a look?'

Holly followed him up the driveway.

The keys of Brother Orange started reaching for a page that wasn't there, words groaning to get out. A message in a bottle, but without the ocean and the cork and the actual bottle.

This was a once-in-no-one's-lifetime-ever opportunity.

They walked up the driveway and around the side of the house. He led the way, climbing over a fallen-down side fence into the overgrown backyard and looking around for his mom. But she wasn't there. He motioned towards the house, led Holly up onto the back verandah, where he pushed a door open. Holly followed him inside.

They were standing in a kitchen that would have been modernised sometime in the 1950s. A set of swinging kitchen doors led them into the loungeroom. It was the strangest thing. All the furniture was still there, as if the last owners had simply stood up and left without packing a single bag. Chairs were pushed back from the dining table; books lay haphazardly on shelves in the lounge room; a velvet sofa sat positioned to face a television cabinet with its glass-fronted doors hanging open. Everything looked decayed and aged and coated in a layer of dust. In front of a smashed floor-to-ceiling window were the skeletal remains of a Christmas tree tipped onto its side, dried-out pine needles carpeting the floor.

It was eerie. There was a sense of the *Titanic* to it.

'What happened?' she asked him. 'Why's everything been left like this?'

'Got a bit of history, this house,' he said. 'Long story.' He called out, 'Mom?' Listened a moment. 'I think she's upstairs. Come and have a look – I've got something to show you.'

Despite the lack of paper, the keys started hammering against the roller, typing words that would never be read, onto a page that hadn't been inserted, possessed with the urgency of what they needed to convey.

Holly. THIS IS IMPORTANT. I found that box you were talking about. The photo from Morocco...

'So what are your parents going to do with the place?' Holly asked, her hand running up the wrought-iron balustrade as they climbed the stairs. 'It needs a lot of work.'

'Yeah,' he said, leading her into a room where heavily brocaded curtains were falling drunkenly off the railing. A mattress had been tilted off the bed, and there were ugly stains on the faded carpet. A large chunk of the ceiling had fallen in and crashed to the ground. One of the bedside tables had an empty space where the top drawer used to be. The other bedside table was tipped onto its side.

...the guy in that photo, he stopped to pick me up the afternoon we swapped. I was hitchhiking, and he pulled over and offered me a lift. There was something about him. I knew I shouldn't get in the car with him. Something was off about him. If he's your dad, you need to stay away from him. He's dangerous. Please write back straight away. I need to know you got this letter. I hope you get it. It's important. Love Trinity

He reached over and stroked her face. 'You're beautiful,' he said. 'You know that.'

Fear descended like snow, dusting Holly's entire being.

In the neonatal intensive care unit at St Anne's, a haze hung over the last humidicrib in the row. Under the plastic cover, the little limbs struggled, the tiny hands curled into fists. The preemie baby with the Rhnull blood type squawked feebly, her heart rate dropping, her breathing becoming erratic.

Holly ran towards the bedroom door, but he got there first. Put his palm against it, keeping it closed. She ran to the window and struggled to get it open. He wandered over and stood beside her, not at all concerned.

'You want help with that?' he asked, taking hold of her wrist as they both looked down to the concrete driveway two storeys below. 'You're more than welcome, if you want to give it a try. You'd take away some of my fun, and I'd have to go find someone else, but honestly, go for it. How's your little sister, by the way?' He shrugged. 'One door closes, another one opens. Or, one window opens, another one opens too.' He smiled at his joke.

Holly struggled to wrench her wrist out of his hold. His grasp slipped and she ran back towards the door, but again he was too quick for her. Too strong. He pushed her up against the door, his arm against her throat. She tried to push him off. Tried to breathe. Tried to think.

'What are you doing?' she managed to get out. She was struggling to make sense of it all. 'What about your mom?'

He stopped for a moment. Frowned.

'What are you talking about? You still don't get it? My mom's not here. They didn't buy the house. There's no builder. It's just you and me, kid.'

But it couldn't be. That couldn't be right. She'd only got in his car because she trusted him.

'You're my dad,' was all she could think of, all she could say.

He laughed, taken by surprise, and the pressure at her throat eased slightly. But there was no dimple. No reward for making him laugh.

'What?' he said. 'Hardly. Old enough to be your older brother, maybe,' and here he laughed again. 'But dad? No. Impossible.'

The pressure on her throat started to increase again. She needed to explain to him. Make him understand. Make him stop.

'The little baby. In St Anne's. Frances's baby. That's me.'

He pulled his head back and looked at her, eyes narrowed. 'What are you talking about?' he said, shaking his head.

'It's true,' she gasped. 'I don't know how it happened, but my name is Holly Fitzgerald. Frances is my mother. You're my father. I'm that baby in the hospital.'

He scoffed. 'Yeah? Well, here's the thing, sweetheart – that baby in the hospital definitely ain't mine.'

The monitor was beeping erratically. A nurse came running in, calling over her shoulder for others. She removed the cover, started pressing against the tiny chest, whispering urgently all the while. 'Holly. Come on, Holly. Stay with us. Stay. Stay.'

Holly's head snapped back as he slapped her, the strength behind his palm jolting her. She wasn't sure why he'd done it. She seemed to be losing track of what was going on.

'Wait, what?' she said, putting up her hands to stop him hitting her again. Repeating the same line and hoping for a different answer, she said: 'But you're my dad.'

'Even if you were that baby all grown up,' he said, as if suddenly he had all the time in the world to amuse her, as if she was going to like this story, 'which is, little lady, only happening in your imagination, I still wouldn't be your father, because that baby ain't mine.'

'But I've seen you. In photos. In Morocco with Frances.'

'Nathan's the one who went to Morocco. Not me. You're talking about my brother.' The mention of Nathan seemed to fill him with strength and anger. He pressed his arm against her windpipe again. 'I don't want you talking about him,' he said. 'You didn't know him. Leave the dead to rest in peace.'

Holly struggled to breathe, struggled to work out what he was saying. She looked into his eyes and saw evil, right there, in their cold depths. There was a strong family resemblance to the photo in Morocco, but now that she was looking with the clarity that near-death brought, she could see how wrong she'd been. She'd seen him that day out the front of the hospital with Frances and had joined the dots to form the picture she wanted to see. But all this time, she'd been wrong. Nathan had been dead all along.

'Besides,' he went on, loosening his chokehold on her slightly, 'it's doubtful that's even Nathan's baby. It could be anyone's.' His mouth turned down as if the thought of Frances made him taste something unpleasant. 'Last week when I picked you up that first time, well...'

Holly blinked at him. This was the guy in the car from that first day. Lewis had heard a crack like thunder and come outside. Trinity had been propelled to safety, forty years into the future. This was the guy who'd driven off.

'I'd just dropped her at the hospital to have the kid,' he went on, 'and there you were, standing with your thumb out, just asking me to pick you up, same as her, same as that piece of trash. Made me so angry.'

His arm was pushing hard on her windpipe again. Holly's vision started closing in from the outside, a black vignette sucking in towards the centre. Everything sounded far away. *Come on, Holly. Stay with us. Stay. Stay.*

'And then you turn up at the hospital on Tuesday, pointing your finger at me, going, "You're here." So yeah. Here I am. Looks like today's your lucky day.'

She wasn't going to get out of here alive. Trinity wasn't going to get out of here alive. Holly had failed in her mission to protect her, to break the evil, to Reset.

Her instincts to protect herself kicked in.

Her and Evie, their feet bare, hands ready at 'yoi'. Prepare yourself.

She took as deep a breath as she could manage, found her centre, and lifted her foot off the floor. She only managed a few centimetres, but she could work with that. She put the outer edge of her foot against his shin, then stomped down as fast and as hard as she could on the fine bones on the top of his foot. It was a standard, and highly effective, karate move.

Instinctively he stepped slightly back from her, flinching from the source of his pain, creating a gap between their bodies. Taking the opportunity, Holly jammed her fist into the unprotected area of his throat. The soft part. He stumbled away from her, coughing, gasping for air. She stepped towards him, put her hands around the back of his head and pulled it downwards, slamming her knee into his nose. He reeled back, hand up to his face, shoulder up as a shield. She hooked her foot around the back of his heel, same as she'd done with Lewis in the kitchen at home, and threw him off balance. He fell to the floor, slamming his head on the edge of the tipped-over bedside table on the way down, then lay still.

Holly nudged him with her toe. He was out cold.

As she stared down at him, the darkness that had been threatening rose up and swept over her. She collapsed unconscious on the floor beside him.

Day 8

**FRIDAY,
7 MARCH
1980**

Trinity

5.16 pm

Trinity Byrne woke up on the floor of a dark, unfamiliar room.

She coughed. Her throat was sandpaper-raw. Her bones felt bruised and her senses were prickling with strangeness. She sat up and looked down at her legs, at her Converse sneakers. She held up her hands in front of her face, then brought forward a hank of her long blonde hair, staring at the black home-dyed tips. She couldn't explain why, but it felt so good to be in her body.

It took a moment for her eyes to adjust to the low light. The door to the room was closed, and she was slammed with a sense of suffocation and terror. She got to her feet unsteadily, then noticed a guy lying unconscious on the floor near the door. She squatted next to him, pushed his cap off his face. She knew this man, but she couldn't think where from.

He groaned slightly, his body starting to stir.

'Are you okay?' she asked.

Who'd done this to them, knocked them both out cold? He was lagging behind her, but he'd be conscious in a minute or two. He could tell her what was going on. Trinity pushed at his shoulder.

'Are you okay?' she repeated.

He grimaced slightly, eyes still closed.

A car had pulled over. The driver had leant over and wound down the passenger-side window. He was wearing a cap and sunglasses, his face in shadow. She said she was going to the Greek – was he going that way? He replied that he was going right past it, so hop in. Something about him had felt off. Maybe she shouldn't get in the car this time. But that would have been rude. She'd stuck her thumb out and he'd offered her a lift – she couldn't very well turn him down now, could she? She opened the passenger door, went to hop in. And then nothing.

She stared down into the guy's face. This was the same guy. Same cap. He hadn't taken her to the Greek.

He'd brought her here. Her instincts had been right –
there *was* something off about him. But what had made
her come with him into this place? She put her hand up
to her throat and felt the rawness there. He'd hurt her.
Choked her, maybe? And then she'd collapsed? But then
what had happened to him? Who'd knocked him out?
She looked around. There was no one else in the room.
Just her and him, alone.

And he was starting to come to.

She needed to move, to get out of here, but his body
blocked the door.

Trinity looked around her frantically. She didn't want
to be stuck in here with this guy, especially not when
he woke up. But what was she supposed to do? He was
putting his hand up to his face, feeling for the headache
that must be swelling inside his skull. Any second now,
he would open his eyes, and then she'd be done for.

There was a chunk of plaster from the ceiling lying
close by. Trinity reached over and picked it up. It was
solid and weighty. She didn't want to do it, didn't like
the idea of hurting another human being, but it was
either her or him. She held the plaster above his head,
then simply let it drop, not watching to see the harm

she'd caused. The 'oof' she heard, and then the silence that followed, told her enough.

She grabbed his ankle and dragged him a little way from the door. He was heavy – she couldn't shift him far. Then she stood up and tried the door. It only opened a small way before it hit his body with a thud. Terrified that at any moment he would reach out and grab her leg, she squeezed herself through the narrow opening and fled down the stairs.

Trinity tried to open the front door, but it wouldn't budge. The carpet had buckled and was jamming it shut tight. Panic rose in her. She looked back, half-expecting to see him lunging down the stairs towards her. She had to get out. Now.

Running into the living room, she saw the skeletal remains of a Christmas tree lying in front of a smashed floor-to-ceiling window. Trinity scrambled to the window and pushed her way through it, barely aware of the shards of glass tearing at her skin and hair.

She ran down the driveway and out onto the street, where a woman and two young children were getting out of a car. 'Help me,' she called out, stumbling towards the woman. 'Get me away from here. Please.'

8.17 pm

Trinity lay in her bed, exhausted, drained. She'd spent hours with the police, trying to answer questions she had no answers for, Mom clutching her bandaged hand, Dad's arm protective around her shoulders.

The doctors had said she was lucky not to have torn any tendons when she'd pulled herself through the smashed window. But from the police's perspective, torn tendons were the least of her problems. They thought the guy in the house might be the Mariposa Murderer. They were going to interview him as soon as the hospital said they could. They'd said she'd well and truly sorted him out, and they were impressed that she'd been able to get away from him – that she'd somehow managed to knock him out cold and get herself to safety.

Trinity shuddered. Mom and Loolah had both offered to sleep with her, but Trinity had wanted to be alone. She felt safe and warm wrapped up in her familiar yellow cocoon. Although everything was slightly off-kilter. All her stuff had been put away. Books were on shelves. The desk was tidy, with Brother Orange sitting there waiting for some poetry to make life better.

She pushed the blankets off and wandered over to the desk. Put her fingers on Brother Orange's keys. Maybe when all the confusion in her head had settled into something she could explain in words, she would write about what had happened. If she could remember what had happened.

Her mom had said this often happened with shock – it was the body's way of protecting itself; a type of amnesia that made you forget the specifics when something bad happened to you. She'd said Trinity might never remember.

But such a big memory loss? Such a chunk of time?

She remembered the guy stopping to see if she wanted a lift. She remembered opening the car door and hesitating; him saying to her, *Sure, I'm going right past the Greek*, which had seemed odd to her – what were the chances of someone stopping to pick her up already planning on driving straight past the place she needed to get to? And then she remembered nothing.

When she'd woken up in that scary house, she'd assumed that instead of driving her to the Greek to meet up with Susie Sioux and April, he'd driven her there and taken her upstairs.

But it turned out it was a whole week later. The seventh of March.

She'd been living her normal life for an entire week and remembered none of it.

'I'm sure I've got a story to tell you,' she said to Brother Orange, feeling the cool keys under her fingertips, 'but I haven't a clue what it is.'

Trinity pulled out her desk chair and sat down. She opened the top drawer of her desk, looking for a sheet of paper to thread into her typewriter, and found a stack of letters; picked one up and started reading. She frowned, put it down, and picked up another one. And another. There were pages of letters, none of which she recognised. Some of them had a frantic tone, others were angry, a few of them seemed like an adult had written them, trying to calm a child. All of them were written this past week, she was sure of it.

The chunk of missing time was here, explained in these letters. But, conversely, they explained nothing. If anything, they made everything even more confusing than before she'd found them. Reading them, she'd swear they were written by two different people, living two different lives. One from the future. One from now. Lives swapped. But of course, that couldn't be right.

Layered through the letters was a sense of remembering. But also, not remembering. Strange images wove together, but there was no clear thread. Trinity felt like if she stepped back she should be able to see a bigger picture, but instead, all the answers were unspooling. The harder she looked, the less she could see.

Day 15

**FRIDAY,
14 MARCH
1980**

10.42 pm

Trinity stood in front of the crowd, the heft of her electric guitar feeling solid, the weight of it keeping her grounded.

All week she'd had a sense that she might float off. So many strange things had happened that she couldn't explain. O'Farrell had expected her to turn up to catch-up classes in the library on Monday. Coach was looking forward to seeing her at softball training on Thursday. And stranger still, she'd decided to go. She felt like she wanted to do these things. She wanted to fold her clothes and put them away each night. She wanted to make her bed each morning. She wanted to go for her nightly runs again. She even wanted to read Asher Lev. (But not to please the Reaper. Never to please her.)

Susie Sioux's house was filled with all their friends, everyone there to celebrate Susie Sioux's birthday. Despite the abduction, despite Mrs Watanabe thinking maybe they should cancel and even Susie Sioux considering postponing, the party had gone ahead. Trinity was happy. She wanted to be here, with her head so full of music she couldn't fit another thought in.

And right now, she and Susie Sioux and April *were* the music, the sounds they were creating tying them together in this moment. The music vibrated through each of them, through every person in the room, the dancing bodies plaited into the tapestry of the songs. Her calloused fingers pounded at the strings of this beautiful guitar. Not a Fender or a Gibson. A Lotus.

She stepped forward and yelled into the microphone, 'This is for Susie Sioux. Happy birthday, Boss,' and she kicked into the tinny riff that ushered in their final song for the night: 'Hong Kong Garden', the inspiration for the transformation of Susan Watanabe into Susie Sioux.

As she sang the last song of their set, Trinity found herself staring across the room at Lewis, who was dancing away. He looked, she realised, exactly like the sort of person a girl would be crazy not to kiss.

As, of course, she'd always known he was.

2.37 am

Trinity and Lewis walked home side by side, their feet keeping lockstep with each other, Trinity feeling pleasantly drunk.

'So you don't remember anything from that week?' Lewis checked, not for the first time, his eyes watching the pavement as if he needed to concentrate on walking a straight line. Maybe he did. They'd certainly had enough drinks to make walking a straight line a test of skill.

'No,' she said. 'I wish I did. It kind of drives me crazy, but Mom says I might never remember.'

'Me coming out and finding you on the footpath?'

'No.'

'Karate-kicking me to the floor in the kitchen, cereal going everywhere?'

He'd asked her this a few times already, and she wished she had a memory of it, because every time she heard about it, it made her laugh.

'No.'

'Catching the baseball? Coming to the art room? Lewis Rodda?'

'No. No. And…no.' He hadn't mentioned that one to her till now. 'Who's Lewis Rodda?'

'No one.'

He plunged his hands in his pockets and looked away. Then he looked back at her. 'Me holding your hand?' he asked.

She put the brakes on, and turned to look up at him. He stopped beside her.

'Wait. When?'

'In the art room.'

'You weren't going all Olivia Newton-John, John Travolta on me, were you?' she teased.

He started walking again, a grim set to his jaw. She raced up to him and grabbed his arm.

'Hang on,' she said. 'I'm joking. I don't remember it. What happened?'

He looked at her as if he didn't quite trust her, and then he took her hand.

'Nothing much. I did this.'

She looked down at their two hands, holding each other. She looked back up at him.

'And then what happened?'

'Then? You let go.'

'You see, that's when you should have known for sure something weird was going on with me.'

'Really? Why? How do you think it should have played out?'

'Oh, I don't know. Maybe something like this,' she said.

And she stepped closer to him, their hands still entwined.

He looked down at her, checking that she wasn't teasing, then moved in towards her, close enough that they were nearly kissing, but not. Only an inch between them.

'And then?' he asked.

And then Trinity made up the rest of the distance. That tiny inch.

Day 86

SATURDAY, 24 MAY 1980

12.01 pm

Trinity's mom and dad sat her and Loolah down. 'We have to tell you girls something,' her mom said, holding her dad's hand.

Trinity watched her parents carefully. When they'd broken up just before Christmas, she hadn't seen it coming, and she still wasn't quite sure why it had happened. But now that they were back together, she was keeping a close eye on them, determined to make sure they stayed together this time around. Ready to step in if need be.

Instead of seeing clues of friction, though, she'd seen clues of forgiveness. The way Dad would look at Mom, like she was a gem and he was never letting her go again. The way Mom had given him a hard time at first, the cold shoulder, but then relented because, after all, if they were going to stay together she couldn't keep punishing him. The way, over the past month or so, they'd all settled into a rhythm that felt right, good, happy, solid. Complete.

Nearly complete.

'Remember that baby, Trinity?' Dad said. 'The one you donated blood to?'

Trinity nodded, because yes, she knew about that baby. She'd read all about her.

Both Rhnull...both broke our collarbones, even. I went to St Anne's yesterday and donated blood. To myself. Blew my mind.

'We've decided to adopt her,' Mom interrupted, Dad's pace too slow for her, his story-telling getting in the way of the punchline.

Trinity's brain went into some kind of transmission breakdown, unable to comprehend the next few sentences. The news was too big, too abstract, too unbelievable. When she finally managed to tune in again, Mom was saying, 'She's the dearest little thing. I mean, I often fall in love with the babies that I help deliver, but this one, she's different. I got to know her mom a bit, before she moved back to Australia. She's only young. Twenty. She wasn't ready to have a baby, and she worried that she wouldn't be able to take good care of her. We discussed it, the three of us – her, me and your dad. She gave us her blessing. The final documentation went through the lawyers yesterday.'

Trinity felt all of her organs plummeting and twirling and beating and spinning. Rearranging. Flipping. She thought she might be sick.

'Maybe we should have spoken to you two about it before now,' Dad said, 'but we wanted to make sure all the 't's were crossed before we told you. We didn't want you getting your hopes up only for it to fall through.'

Tears unexpectedly began to fall down Trinity's cheeks. It had all been there, in the letters. That little preemie baby who had grown up to live a life that wasn't what she wanted.

...everything I've ever been told is a lie. I think that's why we've swapped: so I can fix things and have a better life second time around.

Loolah jumped off the couch and clapped her hands, bouncing on the spot. 'I'm gonna be a big sister!' She threw her arms around Trinity. 'What are you crying about? This is the *best* news!' She ran over to Mom and

Dad and jumped into their faces, knocking Dad's teeth with her excitement and laughing at the pain she'd caused with her exuberance.

'We have a few things to finalise,' Mom said, wiping away tears of her own, 'but we thought we might go down and visit her today. Introduce you girls to your new baby sister.'

Trinity had now shifted up a gear to full-blown, messy sobbing. Mom came over and sat close beside her, rubbing her back. 'We don't have to go today if you don't want,' she said. 'I know it's a lot to take in. Are you okay?'

Trinity wanted to say something, but all her words were too small and ineffectual. They didn't have the capacity to express what her body was feeling. This was so enormous, so huge, so gigantic, so completely and utterly right.

The best she could manage was, 'Yes. See her,' and that right there, those few small words, were about as accurate an expression of what she was feeling as anything.

1.12 pm

At St Anne's, Trinity's mom and dad led the way to a room with blank beige walls and a crib. Very hospital-y.

Inside was a plump-cheeked, blonde baby girl who started giggling and wiggling, holding Loolah's Holly Hobbie doll, reaching with her arms for Trinity's parents to pick her up. Dad leant in and kissed the top of the baby's head, keeping his nose there for an extra moment.

'She knows us pretty well by now,' Mom said, and she hoicked Baby Holly, with doll, onto her hip so that she was facing Trinity and Loolah. 'She'll get to know you girls too real quick, I'm sure of it.'

Trinity held back, suddenly overcome with shyness, while Loolah stepped right up and put her arms out for her baby sister, loving her immediately, without hesitation. Mom put Holly in Loolah's arms, reminding her to hold her head, and Trinity watched as Loolah tenderly bent down and became a big sister in one small movement.

All those letters. From this little baby. Obviously, that couldn't possibly be.

Dad came up beside her and put his arm around her. 'You doing okay?' he asked. 'It's a lot to take in.'

Trinity looked at Mom. At Loolah. At Dad. And, yes, at her little baby sister. Holly. She felt a swelling of something like pride in her chest, at the thought of everything this tiny wee baby had managed. It was no small thing to Reset an entire future, and look at this. Here she was. Mission accomplished.

Loolah looked over at Trinity, then back down at Baby Holly. 'You wanna hold?' she asked.

Trinity hesitated for a fraction of a second, then nodded, holding her hands out. Loolah shuffled the tiny baby body into the crook of Trinity's arm. Little Baby Holly looked up, clear-eyed, and reached a pudgy hand up to Trinity's mouth. Trinity smiled, nibbling on tiny fingers.

'Hey you,' she said to her brand-new sister. 'It's me.'

And, no kidding, she'd swear on her Lotus Strat that little Baby Holly winked right back.

Acknowledgements

If there was more space, these people would absolutely have their names on the front cover alongside mine: Anna McFarlane, Elise Jones and Sucheta Raj. Your intuitive, perceptive, engaged, clever editorial advice was a joy to receive. You gave me the space to go off on any number of tangents and always made me feel safe to explore ideas that may or may not work. Your patience and red pens wrangled this unruly manuscript into an idea that I genuinely enjoyed working on. Also, thanks to copyeditors Sonja Heijn and Hilary Reynolds, who threw in little gems late in the day that surprised and delighted me. To Sandra Nobes and Kim Ekdahl for a cover design that everyone is loving. And of course to the rest of the team at Allen & Unwin, who are always a joy to deal with.

To my early readers – Susan Stevenson, Melody Ducasse, Doone Colless, Anna Robinson, Andrew

Williams and Charlie Williams – who read some truly dreadful drafts of this book. Thank you for your genuine enthusiasm. Read this new version, it's definitely better!

I'm extremely fortunate to work at the independent bookshop Readings, with fantastic staff, great friends, and awesome bosses (a special shout-out to Mark Rubbo and Bernard Vella). Every single day, it's a joy to come to work. My work as the Grants Officer for the Readings Foundation has shown me what compassionate, community-minded corporate governance looks like: ten per cent of all the shop's profits go to the foundation. Bravo, Readings! And my work as the Readings Prize Manager has exposed me to all the amazing debut authors coming up through the ranks, with a special plug for the #OwnVoices movement that's inspired a whole new generation of authors to speak out.

Thanks also go to all the other bookshops and booksellers, book readers and book writers, book bloggers and #LoveOzYA advocates who have been so supportive of me over the years – without you, there is no industry!

To my beautiful and amazing friends, who have been with me through literally every single major event in my life – Alison Marquardt, Kate McCulloch, Lindy Lloyd, Liz Read, Margie Mitchell, Sally Fether, Sarah Larwill,

Simone Lambert and Simonette Varrenti, as well as their assorted partners and children. Love!

Also – dedication at the front, thankyou at the back – thanks to Andrew, Nique, Harry and Charlie. I love travelling through time with you (albeit in an orderly, linear, un-metaphysical, un-messed-up way).

And one last thankyou: to Brother Orange. I found him in a second-hand shop in Katoomba, and without him, there would be no this.

About the Author

Gabrielle Williams lives in Melbourne and has three kids, one husband and a dog. In the name of research, she has spent time underground with a clandestine group called the Cave Clan, conducted a series of in-depth interviews with a group of notorious art thieves, and spent an inordinate amount of time working out the metaphysics of time travel. She is the author of a number of critically acclaimed young adult novels, namely *Beatle Meets Destiny*, *The Reluctant Hallelujah*, *The Guy, the Girl, the Artist and His Ex* and *My Life as a Hashtag*, all of which have been shortlisted for a number of prestigious awards.